To Jill Bruin

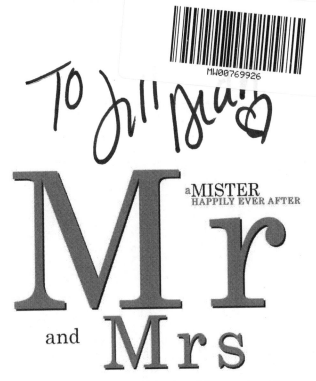

a **MISTER**
HAPPILY EVER AFTER

# Mr

and **Mrs**

New York Times Bestselling Author

# HUSS

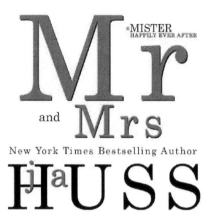

Mr
&MISTER
HAPPILY EVER AFTER

and Mrs

New York Times Bestselling Author

HUSS

Edited by RJ Locksley
Cover Design by JA Huss

## CHAPTER ONE

# FIVE

My queen is scared as she looks out over our little lagoon in the Caribbean. I'm holding her hand, squeezing it tight, anticipating her emotions as they ebb and swell like the waves crashing on our private island beach.

"It's gonna be fine," I whisper into her ear, trying to get my words past the wind.

She nods, but her eyes never leave the horizon.

Mr. Perfect is coming first. I know that much. And while we're both excited about that, he and Ellie aren't the Mr. and Mrs. we're anticipating the most.

It's Cindy she wants to see. And Ariel. And Belle, and Jasmine, and Oliver. And her parents, but it's mostly Cindy and Oliver today. The rest of her family are coming tomorrow night to get ready for the weddings.

We've seen her parents—and Belle—over the past fifteen years. Quite often, actually. Several times a year, but it's never been enough. Jasmine, Ariel, Oliver and Cindy though... she hasn't seen them since she 'died'. She hasn't talked to them. We have strict rules about her safety. I gave her an app back when we cheated death and I hid her away on this island. An app her family could use to talk to her. It's called Dead Notes—a little pun on the Love Notes app I made for her when I was fifteen and we were looking at our first real separation. Her family can call her phone number, hear her voicemail greeting, and then leave a message. If Rory were really dead she'd never get those messages, but it would make the family left behind feel better.

She's not dead. So she did get those messages. And so many of them were filled with tears and sadness, I wanted to take the app away.

Of course I couldn't do that. It was her lifeline to her brother and sisters.

But today... today all those messages from the family she's been missing will come in person. Face to face.

She's scared and I don't blame her. I'm scared too. I kept this secret from Oliver for fifteen years. And yeah, back then he was just a kid. But he's not a kid now.

I think he's gonna kick my ass.

I think I deserve to get my ass kicked.

I think I'm looking forward to it. It's gonna be a relief to bring them all in on our secret.

Then we hear it, the tell-tale sound of a helicopter's rotors echoing off the sky. We can't see it yet, but Rory leans forward just as Isabella and Anastasia, our twelve-year-old twins, come up on either side of us. The younger girls, Mathilda, who is seven, and Louise, who is five, are both back at the house playing. They are still innocent and have no clue why we live on this island.

"Is that them, Daddy?" Isa asks.

"That's them," I say.

"McCallister and Ellie," Ana says. "He's a well-known philanthropist and she's a writer. His net worth is—"

"Stop it, Ana," Isa says. "No one cares what he's worth."

"I just like to have my facts straight," Ana retorts, defensively.

I look over at Rory and catch her smile. Our twins are so different. They aren't even identical. Isa has brown hair and brown eyes, like me, while Ana has blue eyes and blonde hair, like Rory. But Ana is my little analytical girl, while Isa is my little daddy's girl. Given the chance, Ana might take over the world one day—Isa will be content to mother everyone.

If they ever get to leave this island, that is.

They've been all over the world, but only on yachts and private planes, and everywhere we go, we have to skirt around customs. They've been smuggled in and out of more places than I can count. They have more fake birth certificates and passports than I can count and they've never been to school. But they are worldly in every way that counts. They are educated. I've made sure of that. They are fluent in three languages, are well on their way to mastering calculus, and they know how to socialize, even if it's only with the well-hidden children of other outlaws.

Our island is massive by island standards. One hundred and twenty-two acres that holds a good proportion of jungle and cliffs to wander through and climb over, as well as three beaches. We have a stable of ponies—because no daughter of ours could possibly pass through childhood without a pony—and a garage filled with dirt bikes. Because according to their maternal grandfather, every girl needs to know how to ride a bike.

"Look!" Isa exclaims, pointing to the sky. "There it is!"

The helicopter is still a ways off, but it grows bigger as it approaches the island helipad.

Rory squeezes my hand tighter, if that's possible. "Here we go." She sighs.

"Don't worry, Mommy," Isa says, ever looking for an opportunity to comfort someone. She's got Rory's other

3

hand, while Ana stands by her side, shading her eyes from the sun. "Everyone will love us and life will be normal again. You just watch."

We've told them everything. From the very beginning. When they were babies we made it into a fairytale. *You are special princesses, hidden from the world to keep you safe.* But a few years ago we started adding to the story.

*People might want to hurt you, just because of who you are. You have to learn certain skills to keep yourselves safe.*

They studied jujitsu relentlessly since they were old enough to follow instructions. We have a shooting range, and they are both well on the way to mastering that form of self-defense. They have learned to hack, and code, and survive on this island by fishing, and lobstering, and knowing their way around an edible plant. They can sail a boat, are learning to fly my new sea plane, and have taken lessons from their aunt Harper on how to command the crew of a yacht.

I might be turning my little princesses into my older sister, Sasha, but I don't care. I am their father and I *will* keep them safe.

Rory and I don't see eye to eye on that. She wants them in school. She wants them to be cheerleaders, and go to prom, and fill out college applications. I know the only reason she's gone along with my survival-skill-based education is so that one day, probably in a few years, she can point to them and say, "See? They have learned to fly. Now let's let them soar."

But I will say no.

Every. Single. Time.

The helicopter is close now, and a few seconds later it's hovering over the helipad, preparing for landing. It will drop off Mac and Ellie, then go back to wait for Nolan,

Ivy, and baby Bronte. Everyone is coming separately today. West, Tori, and Ethan will come later on their boat. And I'll be leaving to pick up Pax, Cindy, Oliver, and Katya in a few hours. They're over on Pax's island about fifty miles north of here.

We've taken every precaution. Each of the Misters is coming in stealth. Even though there's been no sign of Silver Society activity in almost a year, we're taking no chances.

Tomorrow, our fathers are in charge of getting people here for the wedding.

I smile.

A real wedding with all our families and lots of food. There's a tent set up, and we've flown in a famous band from Amsterdam for music. Ivy Delaney's father is even going to perform the service.

Ivy and Nolan are already married, but they eloped the second he found out she was pregnant. This wedding is a promise he made to her father to make up for that faux pas.

It makes me chuckle to think that Nolan and I actually have something in common aside from the Silver Society. Finally, our queens are getting the wedding they deserve.

We've been waiting so long for this. We've dreamed about it. Fantasized about it. Rory has told me every little detail about how she's always envisioned our wedding and I'm gonna make good on all of it. Right down to our beautiful little princesses being part of it.

We climb the sand dune that leads over to the helipad just in time to see the helicopter touch down. We're all barefoot—our normal footwear for so long, we might've forgotten how to wear shoes—and the twins' long hair blows out behind them in the wind as we get closer.

5

The 'copter door slides open and Mac jumps out first, ducking his head under the spinning rotors. He reaches inside and then Ellie emerges, taking his hand as he helps her down.

I smile, happy to see them again. Even though I don't know them all that well, we've been through some shit together. They feel like family. Having a group wedding with him, Cindy, Oliver, and the rest of the Misters... well, I can't imagine anything more fitting.

I'm walking towards Perfect, my hand outstretched, ready to shake his and pull him in for a man-to-man clap on the back, when someone else appears in the helicopter doorway.

"Who's that?" I ask, more to myself than to Rory.

But Rory answers anyway. "That's Ming," she says over the roar of the helicopter. "Ellie's best friend. She's going to be her maid of honor."

"Oh," I say. I'm surprised. Not that Ellie would want her own maid of honor and not use one of Rory's sisters as a stand-in, but because no one mentioned her to me before this. I know Ivy's fine with Belle acting as her maid of honor. She's become close with all the Shrike sisters since she and Nolan moved away from the resort they run in California and out to Colorado to be close to all the other Mrses. And I know Tori asked Ariel to be her maid of honor—they are thick as thieves and almost always up to no good together. Cindy wanted Jasmine, and Katya didn't want anyone. She has no family left and she felt this was a way to honor the sister she lost and who couldn't be here.

But why didn't I know Ellie was bringing someone? In fact... how the fuck did I miss that there weren't enough Shrike sisters to go around for wedding party stand-ins?

"Did someone do a background check on her?" I ask, irritated at this new development and at my lack of insight.

"I did," Rory says. But it's the way she says it that has me staring at her, waiting for the rest of the explanation. "She's very important to Ellie." Rory stops for a moment, just as Mac approaches to take my still outstretched hand.

"Five," he bellows. "Good to see you again."

"Yeah," I say, shaking his hand and doing the planned back clap. But I'm totally distracted now, Rory's words still echoing in my head.

"Ellie," Mac shouts over the spinning rotors, just as she and Ming get far enough away from the helicopter so it can take off again. "Have you ever seen such adorable little girls?"

He's beaming at my princesses, who are jumping up and down with excitement. We don't get a lot of visitors.

I look at Ellie, sure there's more to this Ming thing, and find her... frowning. But she notices me watching her and the smile appears. She and Rory exchange looks and I catch Rory shaking her head a little out of the corner of my eye.

What the fuck is going on?

"Oh, dear," the Ming person exclaims. "They are perfection. Are you ready for the test, girls?"

"Test?" I say, not understanding. "What test?" I look over at Rory and she's wincing. "What the hell is going on, Ror?"

"Oops," Ming says. "You said you were going to tell him!"

"I was just about to," Rory says.

7

"Tell me what?" I ask, getting frustrated. "What are you talking about?"

"We're taking a test, Daddy. It was a surprise," Isa says.

"Yeah," Ana says, beaming me a smile. "Surprise! We're going to school next year. So Ellie brought Ming to be our entrance exam test proctor. You know, so we can get into a good one."

"You're not going to school," I say.

"Yes," Rory says, looking me straight in the eye. "They are. I've made up my mind and they're taking the secondary school admission test. Ellie, Ming, and I have been planning this for months and you will not interfere."

She locks arms with Ellie and Ming, like they are a team—solid and unbreakable—and they march off over the dune towards the house chatting about... whatever.

I look at Perfect, frowning. "Sorry," he says with a shrug. "I thought you knew."

"Don't be mad, Daddy," Ana says. "It's time to let us go."

And then she and Isa—the little traitors—take off after their mother, firmly on her side.

Because my queen has spoken and to them, her word is law.

CHAPTER TWO

# MAC

Ellie and Ming disappear with… Rory.

It's kinda hard to get used to that idea after hearing Cindy, Ariel, and Oliver talk about their dead sister when all that shit with the Silver Society went down last year. But I'm adjusting.

This island is something else. I mean, I've seen Paxton's islands. The little one and the big one. But this… this is something altogether different. It's not some blown-out bunker or another rich man's idea of getaway paradise. It's… it's like a private resort. Except only one family lives here.

There's a series of bungalows lining the beach we're staying on. Five in all. One for each of us, plus there's several more on the other beach down the coast where families will stay when they arrive tomorrow.

"Why?" I ask Five, turning to look at him. He's staring at the disappearing figures of the women as they make their way towards the bungalow Ming will stay in.

"Why what?" he asks absently.

"Why all…this?" I say, panning my hand to the elaborate setup.

Five turns to me—reluctantly, almost—and shrugs off whatever's bothering him. "We were planning on opening a resort when all this shit blew over."

"Ah," I say. "I see."

"Yeah," Five says, sighing. "Things didn't exactly go

the way we planned."

"Or quite blow over, either. But hey," I offer. Because the dude seems a little distracted by what just happened out by the helipad. I'm not sure what this test shit is all about—Ellie didn't include me in any of her plans. "Things have blown over now. Right?"

"Have they?" Five asks back. "Rory wants to send our kids to school."

"Yeah, and?" I'm not really getting it.

"They could be targets."

"Well." I laugh. "Come on, man. We're all targets. We've been targets. And from what Cindy and Oliver have told the rest of us, you're the reason. But my kids— if I ever have any—will most definitely not be hidden away from the world like this."

"That's because you don't really know how deep this shit runs."

I shrug. "I have a good enough idea. But the way I see it, my kids are far better off in the public eye—far safer— than if no one knew about them. Believe me, I've tried the hiding shit myself after all that college crap. And the only thing it taught me was that I was running. And you know what?" I ask.

"What?" Five says, finally looking me in the eye.

"I'd rather fuckin' fight than run."

He sighs. Shrugs. And then says, "Hey, if you need anything, just pick up that phone. It'll connect to the house and one of us will pick up."

"You got a staff here, Aston?"

"A few," he admits. "Trusted people."

"Cool," I say. But he knows where I'm going with that comment. The only safe secret is the one no one knows about. And if people know he's here, his secret was never safe.

"And we've run background checks on everyone, so we're good there."

"I'm not the one who's worried," I say.

Five says nothing to that. Just walks away, heading in the opposite direction from the one the girls went.

Our bungalow isn't too far, and the journey to it goes by too fast. There's so much to see here. I've been on private islands before, but this feels like a private country.

I wheel our luggage into the room and collapse into the chair, looking for the TV.

No fucking TV. Are you kidding me? These people are really cut off from the world.

I get what he's saying. And I get why he's scared. But they won. They're still here. And the way I see it, if people really want to find you, they find you. There's no way to really hide in this world anymore. I mean, you can try to stay secluded out here in the middle of the ocean. But eventually a satellite passes over or a boat goes by. Someone gets curious. It's an exercise in futility.

Ellie comes through the door with a sigh. She's sweating from the heat—even though it's October, this is the Caribbean, after all—and pulls her wide-brimmed hat off her head, tossing it towards the coffee table. It floats past and lands on the floor, so I pick it up as she collapses next to me.

"What's wrong?" I ask. Because something is definitely wrong. She's been acting weird all week.

"Nothing," she says, kicking her feet up.

I gently grab her legs and pull them into my lap, slipping her shoes off in the process. When my fingers begin their little dance across the high arch of her foot, she relaxes and shoots me a smile. "That feels nice," she

11

says.

"Everything we do this weekend will feel nice, Mrs. Perfect."

She smiles at the name. Even though it comes with all kinds of baggage. "I'm excited about that part," she says.

"What part aren't you excited about?" I ask. "You're not worried about the Silver Society coming back, are you?"

"No," she says. And I'm relieved. Because if she was, I'd have to pay more attention to that kind of thing. But Ellie is an eternal optimist. She's always been upbeat and positive. Even when she left me to find her own way in the world, she did it with the attitude of a fighter. Someone who wants to play and win. Someone who sees everything as an opportunity.

But she's worried about something and I just can't figure it out. "Then what?" I say. "Because this is your wedding, Eloise."

The sound of her full name has her cracking another smile.

"It's gonna be the best day of your life."

With that declaration she pouts.

"What?" I ask.

She looks at me, every semblance of a smile gone. "It's not."

"Why?"

"Because the best day of my life is yet to come and sometimes, Mac, I think that day will never come. That it'll never happen."

"Oh," I say, finally getting it. I slide my hand up her leg and squeeze her knee. "Babe, it's only been a few months. We'll get there."

"You don't know that. We should go see doctors."

I shake my head at her.

"Why?" she demands.

"Because it's premature, Ellie. We've only been trying for a baby since January. It's not fair—"

"It's October, Mac," she says, her tone firm and stern.

"Right. Exactly my point. Ten months is not a problem."

"I think it is," she says, pursing her lips. "I think there's something wrong with me."

"Babe," I say, pulling her into my lap. "There's nothing wrong with you. We're just getting started. And you're probably just stressed about the wedding and stuff. I mean, it's not exactly the best time to get pregnant, right?"

"What's that mean?"

"Nothing. It's just… stressful. And stress…" I shrug. "It does shit to people. Just wait until all this is over and we're back home, all settled in. It'll happen."

"But what if it doesn't, Mac? What if we never get pregnant?"

"Stop," I say. "We're not talking about it right now. This weekend is just about us. Pretty soon we're gonna be parents and then we'll have to wait eighteen years to get this kind of peace again." She makes a face, intent on continuing the argument, but I beat her to it. "You know what we're gonna do?" I say, moving her legs off me so I can stand.

"What?" she asks, her head tilting up to watch me.

God, she's so pretty.

"We're gonna go swim. We're the first ones here and Five told me last week they have a whole other island that we can visit if we want time alone. So that's what we're gonna do. When Nolan and Ivy get here with Bronte"— shit, that just made her frown again. Note to self, don't talk about Nolan's new baby—"well, we won't have another moment to swim naked."

Ellie laughs. "We're not swimming naked."

"The fuck we're not!" I say, grabbing her hand and pulling her to her feet. "We're gonna go find that beach, take all our clothes off, and then I'm gonna fuck you senseless."

I get a real smile at that comment. So I keep going.

"Mrs. Perfect," I say, pulling her close so I can press my lips up to her ear. "I'm gonna make you forget about everything but me this weekend. You watch."

"I don't think you can, Mac—"

But my hand is already slipping up her dress. "This is how it's done, right? This is the whole point of sex. To put babies inside you."

"Stop it." She laughs.

But I got a laugh and a smile. So more dirty talk is coming. "I'm gonna rip your clothes off on that private beach this afternoon, Ellie. And I'm gonna stare at your body. I'm hungry for it. I'm hungry for you in a way I've never felt before. I'm gonna touch you everywhere," I say, my hand sliding between her legs, my fingers already stroking her softly. "And make you forget about everything but us."

I kiss her soft, pliant mouth. Her lips respond, then her hands. She wraps her fingers around my biceps and squeezes, like she never wants to let me go.

"Are you ready?" I ask. "Are you ready for the best day of your life on Sunday? The day I say you're mine and you say I'm yours. And we say it together, in front of everyone who counts. And there's no taking it back, Mrs. Perfect. Because what we have is a once-in-a-lifetime thing, babe. And we know that. We appreciate that. And no matter what happens—babies or not," I say, pulling back from our kiss so I can tilt her chin up with my fingertips and make her—force her to—look me in the eyes for the next part, "no matter what happens, we're gonna be happy because we're gonna be together."

"I know," she says, trying to drop her head and stop my intense stare.

But I don't let her. I keep her right where I put her. In my sight. In my arms. "There's no buts. Not anymore. We're together. And if there's no baby, then we'll go adopt every kid we can find and fill that house up with little people who need us just as much as we need them."

She nods and pulls away. I let her, because she's aiming her cheek for my chest. So I give her what she needs more than my hand stroking her pussy. I give her a hug.

"Tori and West adopted."

"Right," I say. "And see how happy they are? They don't need a biological kid to feel complete and neither do we. We'll do whatever it takes to grow our family, Ellie. But right now, let's just be happy together."

She looks up at me, her eyes welling up with tears. "OK," she says, giving in.

"But in the meantime let's keep trying."

She laughs.

"Because I really am gonna take you to that beach and fuck you senseless before Mr. fucking Romantic gets here, bringing all his drama with him."

I take her hand, lead her out of the bungalow, and we find our way into the jungle. We go forward on faith. Faith that everything is perfect. Everything will be fine. And all we need is each other.

# CHAPTER THREE

# NOLAN

"Isn't this exciting, Bronte?" Ivy is cuddling our baby close to her breast as we all look up at the helicopter approaching.

Bronte looks scared if you ask me. It's her first ride. And to be honest, I'm not sure I like the helicopter idea. "Maybe we should just charter a boat?" I say.

Ivy shoots me a weird look. She doesn't even bother answering because I've offered up this alternative several times and she thinks I'm being ridiculous.

Bronte's mouth opens wide as the helicopter touches down. Her wild blonde hair is flying in the wind because I was in charge of dressing her this morning and I don't know the first thing about taming baby hair for a helicopter ride. I'm just about to point to her and say, "See! She's afraid of it." But her delighted squeal has me shutting up.

It figures.

We had to buy special baby headphones for the ride because the noise level is too much for a six-month-old. I got black ones. With little skulls on them. And while I was at it, I bought her a little flight jacket to match. It has the most badass patches on it.

Ivy looked at her this morning. Looked at me. Back at her. Then said, "She looks like she's starring in the baby version of Top Gun, Nolan."

"Yeah," I said, pretty fucking pleased with myself. "So fucking cool, right?"

Then I got another one of those looks for swearing.

Girls. I don't shake my head as the helicopter door slides open and we walk forward. But I want to.

It's not that I wanted a boy. It just never occurred to me that we'd have a girl. And I do realize—after the fact—that it wasn't rational. In fact, it was kinda stupid. It's just... I don't really know what to do with a little girl. It seems everything in that department belongs to Ivy. She does her hair. She paints her toenails with special baby polish. She buys her dresses and makes her look pretty. She even decorated her room.

I wanted green, man. Celtics green because that's my team. I was even gonna settle for green and white instead of green and black.

But nope. Her room is pink and gray.

I do admit, it was a better option. But Celtics green was a good idea too.

I feel out of my element here. And it's only gonna get worse, right? Baby Bronte will grow up to be pre-teen Bronte. She'll fall in love with some jerk in a boy band and plaster that dumbass's face all over her wall. Ivy will take her to stupid boy-band concerts and shit. Then she'll fall in love with a real guy and I'll be the asshole dad meeting her date at the door with a shotgun.

And Ivy is already talking about baby dance classes when she's three.

I think she'd dig tee-ball way more than stupid ballet, but what do I know?

I just don't see how I can win at this daughter stuff.

And I know Ivy's not ready for another one yet, but I'm totally into trying for number two like right the fuck now.

We get settled into the 'copter and Bronte is fascinated by everything.

Wrong again, Nolan. She loves it.

Ivy chats with the pilot for the whole twenty-minute ride. I think about the wedding. Then I remember Pastor Rockwell, Ivy's father, who kinda hates my guts and is gonna be here tomorrow night when all the parents and family show up.

I get it. I took his daughter away. I eloped with her, robbed him and Mrs. Rockwell of a wedding, and then showed up on his doorstep with my newly pregnant wife. He definitely hates me. But it's been over a year, man. Come on. This guy needs to cut me a break.

Our resort out in the California desert is going so well we moved to Colorado so Ellie and Ivy could be BFFs. That's like… a whole three hours closer to Ivy's parents now, since they're still living at that private school he runs up in Massachusetts. They could at least give me that.

Plus I'm making bank now. I was making bank before too, but now it's totally legit bank. Club money is kinda dirty. But resort money, now that's something you can talk to your in-laws about. And I got a huge inheritance when my father passed away last year.

Except Ivy's father isn't into money. He's not impressed by material things.

Which makes me roll my eyes.

"Why are you rolling your eyes?" Ivy asks in the headset.

"Thinking about your dad," I say. "And how I can't ever please him."

19

"Well, he was certainly excited about coming out here for the wedding."

Yeah. But that's because he doesn't know we're all still lying low after we almost got sucked into some bullshit secret society last year. And Five. Jesus Christ. He's gonna ask a million questions about Five and then what do we say?

I don't say any of this to Ivy, of course. Mostly because I don't know this pilot, even though he's on Five's payroll, and he can hear everything we're saying. But also because I don't want Ivy thinking about last year. She got shot.

Shot.

I still can't believe it.

The only good thing to come out of that whole nightmare was that her ex, Richard, was proven to be a douchebag. Which made me look a whole lot better in the eyes of Pastor Rockwell.

Bronte reaches for me, which makes me smile and forget all the crap rolling around in my head as I take her from Ivy's arms. She pats her hands on my cheeks and spits up right on my shirt.

I kiss her chubby cheek and say, "You did that on purpose, didn't you?"

She laughs out her confirmation.

"I think she looks adorable in this Top Gun outfit."

Ivy drags her eyes off the view of paradise below and gives me an indulgent smile. "She does," she says. "But wait until you see her in the special dress I had made for the wedding."

Yeah, that thing. I have no clue where to start with that. I'm really hoping Ivy's gonna dress her for the wedding because it's got like... layers and shit. Tulle or chiffon.

Whatever the hell you call that floofy fabric that fancy dresses are made of.

"And her hair will be so cute!" Ivy squeals. "I can't wait. I'm gonna burn the entire day into my mind and think about it constantly for the next hundred years!"

I thought I knew women, ya know? Thought I had a pretty good understanding of what they're all about. But it turns out I only knew a certain type of woman. Baby girls... I just have no clue, man. None.

Bronte falls asleep soon after that, which makes me feel all warm and happy inside. So I let all the doubts and weird shit crawling around inside my brain fall away and just enjoy the ride.

It is beautiful. The islands down below are nothing but small patches of white sand beaches. The water is so fucking blue—so many unreal colors of blue, there's not even a word to describe it.

And then Five's place comes into view. I've never been here before. None of us have. Five is freakishly weird about letting people on his island. But his queen wanted a wedding, and he knew the rest of us were talking about a group one, so he offered.

I'm kinda humbled that he's doing this, actually. And not only is he allowing the Rockwells to attend, he even invited Pastor Rockwell to officiate.

It means something. Especially to a gang of guys like we are. Tight-knit and filled with secrets. But Five's secrets are part of it, so it means he's one of us now.

I kinda like having a number six on this team. In fact, we're not really six, we're twelve. All the girls are part of us now too. Even his girl—Rory Shrike.

Match is gonna flip his lid when he gets here. And Cindy... Jesus. I don't know what Mysterious has been telling her all these months, but I'm guessing she kicked his ass when he finally broke it to her that her sister was alive.

Cindy and Oliver were kept in the dark on purpose. Five didn't want to risk anyone finding out about Rory. Did I mention he's a little bit paranoid?

He is. And that reunion between Oliver, Cindy, and Rory—not to mention Ariel, who didn't know anything either—well, I wouldn't miss that for the world.

I'm looking forward to my wedding too. Just like Ivy said, I'm gonna burn that day into my mind and think of it often over the next hundred years just like my Mrs. But tonight, when these Shrike siblings all get back together… well, let's just say the shit is gonna go down.

And that'll be one for the books too.

I smile at my private thoughts as the helicopter circles over an island down below. It's big, as far as islands go. I count three houses, a few outbuildings, too many bungalows to count, and something that looks like a barn with paddocks filled with horses, with a whole maze of trails leading into the jungle.

"Yeah," I say, whispering into my headset so Ivy can hear. "We're having a wedding in paradise, babe. There's never been a wedding quite like this before, has there?"

Ivy leans into me, her head resting on my shoulder. "Never before. Never again. We've got the market cornered on best wedding for all eternity. And I can't wait to see you all dressed up in your tux. All hot and sexy." She turns a little, and I think she's forgotten that the pilot can hear her, but before I can warn her, she says, "I'm gonna give you the fantasy night you've always dreamed of, Mr. Romantic."

I look up at the cockpit and catch the smirk on the pilot's face as he looks over his shoulder at us. I pull my headset down with the one free hand Bronte isn't monopolizing right now, and then do the same for hers, so I can lean into her neck and whisper, "Mrs. Romantic, I don't need the fantasy anymore. Because I've got the real fucking deal every day of my life."

She giggles, hiding her face in that shy way she used to do more often when we first met.

And I decide I like that. I miss it.

So I'm gonna make it my goal for our wedding night.

I'm gonna take her to our room, do things to her she's never even dreamed of, and make my Mrs. blush the entire fucking time..

# CHAPTER FOUR

# WEST

I like the boat.

I like Tori and Ethan.

And I like the fact that we're getting married in a few days and Ethan gets to be my best man.

But other than that... yeah. I'm not too excited about this reunion. For one, it's on Five's island and ever since Match explained all the particulars that surround that guy I've been a little leery of him.

He's got history. Not the good kind.

Secondly, is it really a good idea to get the six of us— not to mention our girls—all together on the same small island? Nolan's bringing his new baby and I've got my son with me.

I mean, does it take a genius to figure out that answer?

So I'm not excited about that. But Tori is. She says it's not any different than us moving to Colorado. And I guess she's got a point there. We all live there now. All except Five.

Tori and I sold our house six months ago and bought a place in Fort Collins. It's not down the street from Ariel's milkshake mansion on Mountain Avenue, but it's still too close if you ask me. They are together all the time.

I'm still headhunting, and Tori is my partner now. So she works too. We bought a small jet to fly in and out of Fort Collins airport with the leftover money from the sale of the house. It was a huge gamble after I lost pretty much everything last year. But we've been steadily making it back, so yeah. That's worked out better than expected.

Plus, I kinda like seeing everyone. It's funny—I see Nolan more than I do Pax or Oliver, even though they both live in the same town. Nolan lives down near Denver by Mac's house. But I see a lot of clients down in the tech center, so I stop by their house all the time.

If you'd have asked me last year if Nolan would be my best friend I'd have laughed.

"What are you laughing about?" Tori asks.

"Nothing," I say, stifling my smile.

"Are we almost there?"

"About ten minutes maybe. I think that's it." I point off in the distance to a barely perceptible island on the horizon. "See it?"

Tori squints then nods. "I'm gonna go wake Ethan up and get him ready." She stands up from her chair, leans in to kiss me on the back of the neck—which drives me crazy—then disappears down to the cabins.

I'm ready for this wedding. There was no talking the girls out of a group wedding after things settled down last winter. We've been waiting on Nolan and Ivy to set the date because she refused to walk down the aisle pregnant. She is, after all, a pastor's daughter and they did, after all, elope and not tell anyone.

So we've been shacking up this past year. But Ethan deserves a set of married parents. He's had enough instability in his life. And I like the idea of marriage. A lot.

It means Mrs. Corporate can't get away from me again.

Well, not easily.

I laugh again.

Fucking Victoria. I gave up on us a while back, but last year changed everything for me. And if there's one good thing about coming back to the Caribbean, it's that I am reminded of the time we spent out here on Pax's islands.

It was fucked up, but Jesus, it was fun too. And it got things moving, ya know?

Before that little adventure we were enemies. And after... we were teammates.

Having Five strand us on that island was the best thing that ever happened to me. It was the first time I ever thought about telling the truth. To anyone, but most importantly, to Victoria. How did I ever expect her to trust me when my life was nothing but secrets?

Of course, what followed—all the revelations and finding out my parents were the ones responsible for just about every bad thing that ever happened to me—that sucked.

But you can't move on until you confront all the old demons. I know that better than anyone.

The guidance system on the boat begins beeping, letting me know our destination is approaching.

I take control and steer the forty-foot Sea Ray Sundancer towards the marina and lose track of the past as I concentrate on the future.

Five is there on the dock with Mac and Nolan. They walk up and Five takes over, jumping aboard to get us moored. I step down into the main parlor just as Tori appears from the lower deck with Ethan, his hair all mussed and his eyes still filled with sleep. We've been on the water for the past week—swimming, snorkeling, and diving so I could show him the best place to catch lobsters—so he's understandably tired. But he won't be tired for long. That's not the kind of kid he is.

It was Five's idea for us to buy the boat in North Carolina, dock it there for a few months, then schedule a family vacation to Florida this week. So we motored down the coast and we've been island-hopping all week.

It's overkill. I think we all agree that it's overkill.

But overkill isn't necessarily a bad thing after all we've been through.

I step outside into the tropical heat and sun with my family and Five greets us with a huge smile.

"Victoria," he says, nodding his head at her.

"Aston," she shoots back. Tori is a champion grudge-holder. And she still hasn't gotten over the fact that Five was sneaky. But she's amicable. For Tori.

"Hey, Ethan," Five says to my son.

Ethan runs past him and jumps onto the dock, then takes off running like he's been here a million times, the sleepiness forgotten.

Kids. They just adapt.

I know that better than anyone.

"Where's Ivy and Ellie?" Tori asks, as soon as we're on the dock with Mac and Nolan.

"Over at the main house," Nolan says, pointing.

"I can't wait to see that adorable baby!" Tori winks at him. She has fallen in love with Bronte. We've seen her at least once a week since she's been born. Tori is obsessed. "And..." Tori says, looking up at me with a smile.

I smile back, because I know what she's gonna say. We've been dying to tell everyone.

"We have news to tell." Tori sings that sentence out like she's a giddy little girl.

God, I love her.

"Wait," Mac says, eyeing me. "What kind of news?"

"We're pregnant!" Tori bursts out. "Yup!" she says, holding her hand over her heart. "I've been holding that in for two months!"

"Congrats!" Nolan says, clapping me on the back.

"That's great!" Five says, shaking my hand.

"Thanks," I say. But I'm looking at Mac. Because he's frowning. "What's wrong?" I ask him.

"Ellie doesn't know this," he says. Not like a question, either.

"Nope!" Tori says. "It's news for everyone. I think this is the perfect weekend to celebrate, don't you?"

"Well," Mac says, rubbing his hand down his face. "The thing is..."

"Shit," Tori says, changing her tone. "Don't tell me you guys have been trying and haven't—"

She doesn't have to finish. Mac nods his confirmation. "She's devastated today. And I sorta used you guys as an example of how we didn't need biological children. How great it would be to adopt."

"Shit," Tori says again. This time she looks up at me. "We can't say anything. Not this weekend, West. It will just make her sad."

"Hey," I say. "I'm cool with that. No one deserves to be sad on their wedding day. It can wait."

I'd really like to brag about this baby this weekend, but not because I want to make people feel bad. Just to, you know, be a fucking dude proud of his boys getting the job done.

"You're the best," she says, leaning up to kiss me on the cheek. "I'd better go find our wild son before he disappears into the jungle."

She laughs as she says it, but there's truth in that. Ethan is all fucking boy. From top to bottom, that kid does nothing but jump, and run, and everything you can do with a ball. Throw it, kick it, hit it... he does it all.

I watch her walk off, her round hips swaying

underneath her lilac wrap, her back tanned golden brown from being in the sun this past week.

"Shit, man," Nolan says. "I didn't know it was like… a thing. Does Ivy know?"

"No," Mac says. "And don't say anything. I don't want Ellie dwelling on it this week. I just want her to have a good time."

"Is she gonna be sad to see Bronte?" Nolan asks.

Mac just shrugs. "I wish I could say no, but… dude, I don't know. She's just fucking sad about this kid stuff."

"But you can adopt," I say. "I bet Tori can help you guys find a great kid who would love to grow up with you as his rich bastard father."

I grab his shoulder so he knows I'm just fucking with him. Mac will be a great father. Probably the best ever.

"Thanks," Mac says. "We really should look into that. I don't want her to be so preoccupied with this. Besides, we've only been trying for ten months. How long did you and Tori try?"

I wince, then shrug. "Does it really matter?"

"I'll take that as you weren't even trying," Mac says, sighing. Then he jacks his thumb in the direction of Nolan. "Neither was this asshole."

"Don't worry," Five says. "We won't say anything, right, guys?"

We all nod.

"We'll make sure Ellie has the best wedding ever," I say.

Because we're still the Misters. So if Perfect has a problem, we all have a problem.

# CHAPTER FIVE

# PAX

"Miss Cookie," I say, my hand on Cindy's breast.

"Yes, Detective Mysterious?" she purrs back, her ass grinding into my dick as I press her against the wall of our little island hut.

"I wanna fuck you."

"I know you do," she coos, turning to place her cool hand on my cheek. She pouts her lips at me, movie-star style. "But we're due at the dock in seventeen minutes."

"Seventeen," I growl, my hand paused mid-nipple squeeze as I consider if seventeen minutes is enough time to have a proper fuck, or if this will have to be a quickie.

"Quickie," she says, reading my mind. "We can't be late."

"All right." I sigh. "Fine," I say, pulling her top down and taking both her breasts in my hands. "But we won't have time to roleplay."

"I think I'll live, Detective," she giggles back.

"Except..." I say, kissing her neck. She loves this, so she throws her head back, her long, golden hair falling with it. She's like a goddamned goddess.

"Except what?" she whispers back.

"Except that report you turned in last week, Miss Cookie..."

"Yeah," she says. "The one with my monthly expenses on it?"

"That's the one," I say, kissing her mouth.

"What about it?" she says, her words getting caught up in our kiss.

"It had a suspicious charge," I say.

"Did it?" she breathes.

"Yeah."

"What was suspicious about it?"

"You spent seventeen hundred dollars at a place called the Sugar Stop."

"And?" she says, holding in her giggle as my hand wanders between her legs.

"I'm thinking…" She reaches down to grab my growing cock and I have to pause for a second so I can enjoy it. "I really like how you smell like sugar, Miss Cookie. But seventeen hundred dollars in sweets might be excessive."

"Oh?" she asks in her fake starlet voice. "Well, you're right. It is. But the Sugar Stop doesn't sell sweets, Detective."

"No?" I ask, dropping to my knees as I lift up her short skirt. She's got a bikini on under her little dress. We almost never wear clothes when we're out here on our island, but Oliver and Katya are here too, so…

"No," she says, her fingertips mussing up my hair as I pull her bikini bottoms aside and lick her. She wiggles, leaning back against the wall, like she might need it to hold her up. "They sell sex toys."

I laugh as I lick her. I can't help it. Cinderella Shrike

has the best imagination.

Best. Imagination.

"Would you like an itemized list, Detective Mysterious?"

"Why, yes," I say. "Tell me exactly what you purchased, Miss Cookie. And explain how it's pertinent to your job as my assistant."

"Ohhh," she moans as I start strumming her clit. "Well…" She loses her train of thought for a second, but I reach up and pinch her nipple and she squeaks out, "It's a long list."

God, I love her. "I have fifteen minutes, Miss Cookie. Begin."

"Well," she says, opening her legs to give me better access. I hold both her thighs as I press my tongue into her sweet spot and she grips my hair tighter. "The first thing was the I Rub My Duckie massager."

I stop what I'm doing to look up at her. She's biting her lip, trying not to smile. "What does it do?"

"It's just a fun bath toy. I was gonna surprise you tonight."

"OK," I say, smiling. "What else?"

She pushes my head back between her legs and says, "Don't interrupt me, Detective. I hate it when you lose your train of thought. It's been proven that multitasking is inherently bad for working relationships."

There's no way she can't feel my smile against her wet pussy.

"I just went in for that, but then I saw the Eiffel Tower dildo, and it reminded me of the trip you took me on for Valentine's Day last year. So I had to have it."

"Jesus," I mumble. I back away, grab her hand, and push it between her legs so she can put on a little show for me. "What else did you buy?"

I'm watching her face, not her hand. Because I just love the way she chews on her lip when she masturbates.

"Cookie dough edible lubricant," she says, her words coming out in halting gasps as her fingers get busy. "I can't wait for you to lick it off my ass."

I have my hand inside my pants after that. My fist wrapped around my cock.

"Then I saw the Princessa vibrator."

"Princessa?" I ask, trying to figure out just what the fuck that might look like.

"It looks like a crown," she purrs, reading my mind. "And it spins!"

"Is this shit all real?" I ask, getting a little excited about her imaginary trip to the Sugar Stop.

"Pax." She laughs. "Don't interrupt me. And don't make me work so hard. This is my quickie, remember?"

She pushes my face between her legs again. But fuck this. I grab both her wrists, hike them over her head, press her against the wall, and push my hard dick up against her belly.

"I think, Miss Cookie," I say, staring down into her blue eyes, "such an excessive sex toy bill means you're planning on trying to seduce me."

She says, "Fuck me, Pax. Right now." She tears at my jeans, popping the button open and unzipping me.

"Doesn't it?" I ask, ripping open her shirt and tearing

34

it down the middle.

"Fuck me," she repeats, grabbing hold of my cock and squeezing it with her tiny hand.

I reach for her little bikini bottoms and drag them down her legs, then grab her, right behind both knees, and hike her legs up so I can slide right up inside her.

"Yes," she says. "It's excessive, Detective. Punish me. Right now!"

I thrust inside her and she squeals again. Her hands are all over my hair, her fingertips grabbing onto it, harder and harder as I slap her ass against the wall each time I enter her.

"Fuck me," she whispers. "Don't stop. Ever. Just—"

I kiss her. Hard. Punishing her that way too. I nip her lip as I fuck her against the wall. "I want to see all those toys, Miss Cookie. And I want you to show me how to use them."

"Even," she pants, "even the Eiffel Tower dildo?"

"Especially the Eiffel Tower dildo," I say. I'm fucking her so hard now, her ass is making thumping noises each time she hits the wall.

"Hey!" Oliver calls from the hallway. "What the fuck?"

Cindy and I cup a hand over each other's mouths, stifling the laughs. "Shhh," she says from the other side of my palm.

"Get the fuck out here!" Oliver yells. "We're leaving in five minutes!"

I take my hand away and Cindy calls out, "Be right

there, Ollie! I just gotta grab my curling iron. Go find Pax. I think he's down at the beach already."

"Fuck you. Ya liars. I know he's in there!" Oliver pounds on the door again. "Get your ass out here, Mysterious! Or I'm gonna—"

But then we hear Katya. "Oliver! Stop it! Leave them alone!"

We laugh as Oliver is dragged away, still threatening me.

"Hurry," Cindy whispers. "I'm not letting you go until we come. So hurry."

Oliver is gonna kill me. But hell, Oliver always wants to kill me when we're all together these days. So fuck it. I pick Cindy up, walk her over to the bed, throw her down, and say, "Turn over, Miss Cookie. I'm gonna punish you now."

I spank her ass red and she squeals with delight for every single slap.

And then I grab her hips, push my rock-hard dick inside her again, and fuck her hard until we both come and collapse into the bed covers.

I love this girl. We're getting married in two days and she's gonna be mine forever.

So fuck Oliver. He's just gonna have to get used to it.

# CHAPTER SIX

# OLLIE

Pax's island was a goddamned mess after all that shit went down with West and Tori last year. The other island, which I can see from this beach, was also blown up. But he took it better than I expected. He hired a demolition crew to come out, take down whatever was left standing, and raze it to the ground. It took out a lot of trees too, but he filled it back up with sand

Pristine, white sand.

I think these two islands are worth more now with nothing but palapas and huts than they were with those two houses.

Katya and I just got here this morning, but Pax and Cindy have been here for about a week. Their hut is pretty nice. It's got solar power and running water from a giant cistern. It's even got a ceiling fan.

But the only thing I can think about is… he's in that hut fucking my *sister.*

While I'm out *here.*

"What he's doing breaks all the rules," I snarl at Katya. She does one of those backward motions with her head. Taken aback, I think that's called. "Sorry," I say, trying to pull her close as she drags me down the beach. "It's just… he knows this drives me crazy and he does it anyway. She's my baby sister!"

"And in two days she'll be his wife, Oliver. You need to let it go because he's here to stay."

"I know." I sigh. "I know," I say again. Like I'm trying to convince myself. "But I only have one baby sister. One. Why the fuck did he have to fall in love with her?"

"Well," Kat says as we stop at the dock to wait for Five to come pick us up. "It's my understanding she sorta stalked his ass. She wanted him so she went and took him. I mean look, she's your sister. That alone is enough to explain why they're together. But beyond that, they're just soulmates. You can't stop that, even if you want to. You can't."

I sink to my knees in the sand and pull her down with me. "And on top of all that, fucking Five has been keeping secrets from me too! It's like... it's like I don't even know these people. I mean, my sister was alive all those—"

"Your parents kept that secret too," Kat says, interrupting my rant. "And Sparrow, and Kate."

"I know!" I say. "See what I mean? Who are these people? I don't know any of them. Not really. What do I know, Kat? Tell me. What do I know about them?"

"Well," Kat says, looking out at the ocean. It's a beautiful day. Sunny and warm, but not too hot. There's a nice ocean breeze and the water is the color of paradise. "You know they're family. And I guess that's all you need to know. I think you should count yourself lucky if you truly know one person in your life. It's impossible to really know people unless you're sharing things on a very consistent basis. I understand that better than anyone. It was a mistake to leave my sister alone all those years. It was a mistake to depend on some institution to take care of her. And now she's gone."

Well, shit. I rub my hand down my face and let out a long breath of air. "Sorry," I say. "I know you miss her."

"No," Katya says, turning her head to look at me. "No. I don't miss her."

"What?" I ask.

"I didn't even know her. I don't miss her at all, Oliver. I think that's probably the most disturbing thing I've ever realized about myself."

I... have no idea what to say to that. So I just stare down the beach at the dock.

So many things are happening right now. Now, as in like in this very moment.

Pax is fucking my baby sister in that hut over there, Katya is coming to some false realization about herself, Five is in his plane, on his way to pick us up. My parents are probably at home on the farm, packing for this trip. Two daughters getting married on the same day.

It's some kind of event, right? Huge milestone.

Pax's mother is doing the same. Hell, even Nolan's mother is coming. And Ivy's parents. Five's mom and dad are bringing Kate and his little brother and sister. Even the infamous Sasha is showing up. And her FBI husband, Jax. James and Harper will be here with my cousins. Even Merc is coming to this thing. Not to mention all my sisters.

It's a big. Fucking. Deal.

Right now, all those people are thinking about this trip. Thinking about me and Kat. And all the other Misters. Thinking about why we have to hide out here in the middle of the ocean, thinking about how we'll all be together, in one place, for the first time ever. Thinking about the risk that comes with this celebration.

"You do miss her," I finally say.

"No." Katya shakes her head. "I feel nothing. Not sad, not broken. Not anything. In fact," she says, wrapping her arm around my biceps as she turns, "I feel better than ever, Oliver. I'm glad it's over. I'm glad we won. I'm glad we're here together. I'm glad you're going to marry me. But most of all, I'm glad she's not here."

I just stare at her.

"Because she'd ruin it."

"How, Katya?"

She frowns, shakes her head. "She didn't love me. Me being her sister meant nothing to her. Yeah"—she sighs, waving her hand over towards the hut where Pax is fucking Cindy—"that's kinda rude." She smiles at me. "But… you love him. He's your best friend. He loves you back, even though he probably won't ever admit it. He's not doing it to hurt you, Oliver. He's doing it because he loves *her*. It's really got nothing to do with you at all."

"Hmm," I say, staring at the hut. "Maybe. But what's that got to do with you and your sister?"

"Everything she did when I came back to town was done to hurt me. So I'm not going to miss her. I don't need family like that. If that's what family is, then I don't need it."

I lean into her, wrap my arm around her shoulder, and pull her close. "That's not what family is, Kat."

"I know," she says, smiling up at me. "This is family. So just get over it, Ollie. Let them have their fun."

She's right. So I roll my eyes and sigh real loud. "Fine. I'm over it."

And then she snuggles into my embrace and then points off into the distance as a pod of dolphins swim by.

"You know what I'm really looking forward to?" I ask, staring at the dolphins as they rise and dive to show us their fins.

"What?"

"Seeing Rory and Five together again." I laugh a little. "They were meant to be together."

"I have to admit," Katya says, "I'm a little surprised that you took that news so well. If someone came at me and said my dead sister was actually alive, I'd kinda freak out."

"Yeah, but I never bought into it. I can't tell you why. I can't point to like, one thing and say, 'This is why I never believed she was dead.' I just… I just knew Five would never let it happen, ya know? That if Rory was in that kind of danger, and things went wrong and she got hurt, he'd never stop until he got his revenge. So there's no way he'd go back to London, start a business, and turn flying sea planes into his favorite hobby. But it'd be delusional to dwell on that kind of thing, right? Illogical as well. So I just told myself, 'OK, she's gone. And I'll probably never see her again.' But never say never."

"Never say never," Katya sighs back at me.

"Look!" I say, pointing to the sky. "There he is, right on time."

Fucking Five Aston. You really can set your watch to that guy. Always shows up when he's supposed to.

"Pax!" I yell, pulling Katya up from the sand with me. "Put it back in your pants, asshole. And let's fucking *go*!"

We walk over to the stack of luggage piled up on the dock just as Pax and Cindy come running out of their hut. His hair is all messed up, her top is all crooked, and I'm just about to open my mouth and say something about that shit when Katya leans in and kisses me on the neck. "Let it go," she says. "Just let it go."

I take a deep breath, huff out my frustration, and see them for what they are.

Just two people in love. That's all this is. Just love.

41

# CHAPTER SEVEN

# FIVE

I can see them on the beach as I come towards the island. Oliver and Katya, who I've only met once, and that was before we decided to come clean about Rory being alive.

Oliver is like a brother. Even more so than my real brother, Wyatt, who is almost sixteen years younger than me. I guess that's how Rory feels about my sister, Kate. She's more of a sister than her own little sister Cindy ever was. Cindy was only six when we faked Rory's death to keep her safe, and four of those years Rory was away at Princeton. So they barely saw each other.

I think if there weren't so many Shrike girls, it would've been different. But Oliver really is Cindy's closest sibling.

The next time I look down, there they are.

Ollie and Cindy, together. Waiting for me to take them to their long-lost sister.

He's gonna hit me hard over this bullshit. It doesn't matter what I say, how I explain it, or what excuse I put up—he's not gonna miss this chance to get even with me for lying.

So I'm ready for it as I land the plane on the water and glide up to the dock.

They have a lot of luggage, but it's a wedding, after all. The dresses were sent ahead last week. All five of them. Rory's mom, Veronica, made her dress last year. So she's bringing that with her when the family gets here tomorrow night.

Oliver and Katya reach me first. Pax and Cindy not far behind them. They are all holding hands and I hold that sight in my mind for a few moments before turning the plane off and opening the door.

"Hey, man," Oliver says, taking my hand and pulling me into a tight embrace. "This is fucking great, right?"

He's... smiling? And happy?

I get why he'd be happy. He's marrying the absolutely adorable Katya. But...

"What's wrong?" Ollie says.

"He thinks you're gonna kick his ass," Cindy says, coming up with Pax.

"Dude," Oliver says. "Why the fuck would I hit you? You brought my sister back from the dead!"

"Uh..." I have nothing to say. It's just not the reaction I was expecting.

"So we're outta here?" Pax says. "I got my boat hidden in the interior lagoon. You hear anything about any bad weather coming? I don't want it to get banged up while we're gone."

Now we're talking about the weather?

"It's the nicest fucking yacht I've ever owned and I'm thinking I'd like to keep it a while."

"Nah," I say, snapping out of it. "It's gonna be hot and sunny for the next week."

"Cool," Pax says, pushing past me. "Let's fucking go."

He helps Cindy into the new plane—seats eight now. It's practically a flying boat. The best on the market today and can take off and land on a runway or water. I could probably start a little tourist business if I wanted.

Ollie helps Katya. They claim the last row and immediately begin to chat as we load up the luggage.

"Nice piece of ass you got here," Pax says.

"Yeah," Ollie concurs. "We should get one of these, huh, Pax?" He slaps me on the back. "Why you so quiet, Five? Tell me all about this island you have. Is it better than Pax's? Because if so, he's gonna try to talk me into going in on another one with him, you watch."

Yeah. First he's happy to see me, then we're talking weather, now he's chatting up Mysterious about adding a plane and an island to their collection of shared shit.

What the fuck is going on with him?

"Well," I start, trying to shake off the feeling that something is very wrong with Oliver Shrike right now. "It's a hundred and twenty-two acres—"

Pax whistles at that, then he and Oliver exchange a look of mutual envy.

"—and it's got…"

I rattle off all the specifics. The houses, the barn, the horses, the trails, the bikes.

"Bikes!" Ollie says. "Fuck, yeah, we're gonna ride this weekend, brother. You got enough for all of us?"

"Nah," I say, letting myself relax a little. Maybe he's gonna be reasonable? "They're mostly for the kids."

"Kids." Oliver laughs. "Jesus. I'm an uncle again. I cannot wait to see those little princesses."

"I guess you shoot girls, huh, Five?" Pax laughs. "Like Cindy's father."

"Hey," Cindy says from the back. "You better shoot some girls too, Paxton Vance. I want a whole pack of princesses!"

"Speaking of princesses," Katya says. "Nolan and Ivy brought baby Bronte, right?"

And that's how it goes for the entire ride back to the island. No, Why the fuck did you lie to me? No angry outbursts. No playing the blame game.

Just normal, everyday life.

When we land, all the others are there waiting.

Mac and Ellie. Nolan, Ivy, and Bronte. West, Tori, and Ethan. And of course, my little royal family.

Rory squeals at Cindy and Ollie. They hug and dance and cry happy tears. Isa, Ana, Louise and Mathilda hover at their mother's side, trying to push their way into the fray of joy.

The dogs come up and wag their tails. Hell, a trio of wild pigs even swim up on shore to see what the hell is going on and that makes everyone even happier.

This can't be how it will go. Can it?

Oliver Shrike isn't gonna try to hit me? Kick my ass? Take me down a peg or ten? He's really not harboring some resentment over me taking away his sister?

I can't believe it.

But that's how it's shaking out.

Oliver is gonna be... reasonable.

My eyes won't be black and blue for my wedding photos. There won't be any loud fights over trust and loyalty.

No, I decide. I did it. I pulled it off. This Mister wedding is gonna be the most perfect happily ever after in the history of fairytale endings.

# CHAPTER EIGHT

# MAC

It's been while since all of us have been together. Even longer if you add Five into the mix, because we haven't all seen him since Pax and Cindy had their little run-in with Nolan's sister back in the desert.

So it's nice.

I like these guys. And not in the way I normally like people, which is mostly based on business decisions and mutual agreements on how to get things done. I just... enjoy them.

Nolan is probably the most fucked-up person I've ever met. But look at him now. The only one of us who is already married. And holding that adorable baby girl. If you had asked me a few years ago if Mr. Romantic would ever get married and have kids, I'd have laughed in your face.

Weston should be way more fucked up than he actually is. I mean, his genetic family were all kinds of out there and his adopted family were on their own personally-funded crazy train. Crazy jet. Crazy spaceship. I'd never have pegged Corporate as a second-chance kind of guy. But here he is. Committing to a woman who could probably take him in a fight—business or otherwise.

Paxton. Jesus Christ. Even though he's not nearly as twisted as Nolan, he's definitely the most dangerous of all of us. Mr. Dangerous, they should've called him. He and Oliver have been tight for years, so when I found out Pax had fallen for Ollie's sister, well, I mostly went to that little impromptu meeting at Nolan's resort just to see them fight.

I wasn't disappointed.

Which leaves Oliver. He did fight with Pax over his baby sister, but he's holding it together for now. Probably because of the wedding. Mr. Match is one of those never-see-them-coming kinda guys. You know, the quiet type who snaps one day and decides to lock himself away in a mountain cabin for the rest of his life making his own ammo and living off the land.

But you know what I don't understand—

"Hey," Ellie says, coming up to take my hand and give it a squeeze.

"Hey," I say, letting that thought dissipate as I take in my future wife.

"What're you thinking so hard about?"

"Oh, nothing. Just taking it all in, ya know. It's hard to believe that whole Mister thing might be over."

"Too good to be true," Ellie says, reading my mind.

"Yeah." I sigh.

"It's over. Mac."

I turn my head to look down at her. Ellie is so pretty. She's not seductive like Victoria. And she's not crazy like Cindy. Or even dangerous like Katya or innocent like Ivy. She's just… pretty normal.

I like that. So much.

"You sure about that?" I ask, enjoying her small smile.

She squeezes my hand again. "Goddamned positive."

I huff out a small chuckle. "I'm glad you brought Ming with you."

"Yeah, me too," she says.

"No, I mean… really glad. She's symbolic, right?"

"Is she?" And now it's Ellie's turn to laugh.

"Yeah. Of your life before me. Which was pretty damn good, and that's kinda like a good omen for me. Like your life from now on will be pretty damn good too, because you're bringing the most important parts along with you. Like the book stuff. That next book is gonna be another hit. You really know your way around a self-help plan. I sometimes wonder if I'm taking you off track, ya know? I don't want to do that, Ellie. I want you to be all the things you were before."

"What was I before?" she asks.

"Perfect," I answer back.

"Shit," she says, shaking her head. "I was a fucking mess before you came along."

"Not true. You were the most valuable employee at Stonewall. And if you were still there, you'd probably be vice-president by now."

"Oh, come on." She snorts.

"Ellie," I say, taking both her hands in mine. The sun is just beginning to set, coating the surface of the ocean with a red-gold blanket of ripples. It reflects off her beautiful face. Makes her shine in a way that makes me want to touch her cheek, just to make sure she's real. "You were Mrs. Perfect long before I came along."

She looks away, allowing herself a sweeping smile as she studies the disappearing sun. "You know what that means, right?"

"What?" I ask.

"We really are Mr. and Mrs. Perfect. Soulmates."

"We are," I say, leaning down to kiss her.

I want to say more. Things like... *You're the sweetest thing I've ever laid eyes on.* Or, *You make me better.* Or a thousand other sappy things that men say just before their wedding.

But all that comes out is a promise. "I'm gonna be yours forever."

She stares up at me and frowns. "You don't have to cheer me up, Mac."

"Ellie—"

"You're enough. You're more than enough. I refuse to be sad for things that aren't meant to be. This is a celebration and there's no place for future regrets or past mistakes. Or even present problems. This is our happy time."

"Oh, Ellie, there's so much more to come," I whisper, kissing her soft lips until she opens her mouth to kiss me back.

"Like what?" she sighs back.

"Butter," I say.

We both crack up laughing and everything she just said comes to pass. Because we forget all the future regrets, all the past mistakes, and all the present problems.

"We'll always have the butter." She laughs.

"Always, babe."

# CHAPTER NINE

# NOLAN

"You know what we should do?" I say to Ivy. She's feeding Bronte some freshly pureed bananas picked right off of this fucking island. Rory took her around to all the different orchards they have here and they picked fruit to mash up for my baby daughter.

I kinda love Rory already.

Bronte is gobbling it up like she's never had bananas before. She has, and they're not her favorite unless it comes in the form of banana bread—which also gets mashed up, but mostly by Bronte's chubby little fingers.

"What should we do?" Ivy asks between making goofy faces at the baby.

"We should go on a date. I mean, shit. We've got all these built-in babysitters at our disposal right now. Plus, we're like… in paradise, right? We should definitely go on a date tonight."

"Where?" Ivy laughs, looking over her shoulder at me.

"The beach," I say. "I have a beach fantasy all ready for you. Been planning it for weeks now."

"Really?" she asks, shooting me a coy wink. "Tell me about it."

"No," I say. "That spoils all the fun."

"You mean we don't need a signed contract for this one?"

"You're my wife, Ivy. I know you better than you know yourself. I don't think I need to ask permission anymore."

She raises one eyebrow at me. It's not a cute eyebrow raise, either.

"Not that way," I say. "Get your mind off Martha's Vineyard."

"Good God." She laughs. "I never think about that night."

"Yeah, that fucking Richard. He ruined everything."

"Well, yes. He really did. But…" she says, then pauses for a moment. "Your fantasy was way out of my comfort zone."

"Mine too," I say, suddenly serious. "But that's not what I'm talking about, either. I just mean a good time. Me doing things you like." I waggle my eyebrows at her.

"You mean… like ordinary men?"

"I'm ordinary," I say.

"Nah," she says, shaking her head. "You're very extraordinary, Nolan. But anyway, back to your offer. I think a date night sounds fun. We've barely done anything alone since Bronte was born."

"I know." I sigh. "And I like being with both of you every night. Love it. But I feel like we might've missed out on a few things. We got married so fast. And all that bullshit with the Misters really put a cramp into our honeymoon time."

"Not to mention I was pregnant."

"And that too," I say. I wasn't gonna bring it up, but fuck. Things got serious like… immediately. "A fun night just for us."

"If you can find a sitter."

"Are you kidding? I bet all of them want to sit for us tonight."

"OK. Go set it up and I'll get Bronte to sleep."

I do a silent, *Yes*, with an imaginary fist-pump as I exit our cabaña. I'm gonna take her down to the beach, get her naked, and then…

"Hey!" I yell, noticing West leaving his cabaña with Ethan. "Weston!"

He waves, but barely gives me a second look.

"West!" I yell again, jogging to catch up with him and the kid.

This time he stops, realizing I'm calling his name for a reason that has nothing to do with a greeting—fucking Corporate. Sometimes he's slow on the uptake. "Yeah? What's up?"

"What are you guys up to tonight?" I ask.

"Just taking Ethan down to the beach to throw the ball around." He tosses a football in the air and Ethan, quick little shit that he is, grabs it and then runs off.

"Fun," I say, actually meaning it. "I can't wait until Bronte is old enough to throw a ball around. But that's not gonna be for a while. And right now what I really need is a babysitter. So I can show Ivy a sexy time tonight. What do ya say? Can you guys watch the baby for us?"

"Shit, man," West says, looking at the empty dirt path where Ethan disappeared. "If I can catch him, maybe. And even then, this kid—he's kinda wild, Nolan. Crazy about sports. He's gonna make me toss that ball until it gets too dark to see."

"Cool." I'm weirdly jealous. "How about Tori? She up for some baby Bronte time?"

West looks around, like he's making sure no one's listening. "She can't. She's sick."

"Sick?" I ask. "What's wrong with her?"

"Don't say nothin', OK?"

"Who would I tell?"

"It's pregnancy stuff. I bet it was the boat trip. Dammit, I should've seen that coming."

"Oh," I say, remembering the conversation this morning about Ellie. Welp, I guess I can't ask Ellie to babysit either. "That sucks. Sorry she's not feeling well. But I think I can talk Cindy or Katya into doing it. So no worries. Go have fun with your *boy*."

Did 'boy' just come out sarcastically? No. No. I didn't just do that.

But Weston picks up on it and narrows his eyes. "Did you just—"

"Nope," I say. You don't admit that you really wanted a boy instead of a girl. And you don't get jealous of your friends who do have a boy. It's just not done. So I'm in denial.

"You're sure?" West asks.

"Positive." I blank my face. Like you do in poker.

"You're lying," West says. "You're fucking lying. Ivy doesn't know—"

"No, dude. And I'm not lying. My daughter is the most beautiful baby ever born."

"And you dressed her up in a *Top Gun* outfit for the ride over here."

"That was cool, right?"

West laughs. "Yeah. I fucking loved it. I told Tori we're taking those hand-me-downs and boy or girl, that's how my next kid will dress."

"See," I say. "Ivy just rolled her eyes at me. But I knew it was a great outfit."

"Dad!" Ethan yells from… somewhere. "Come on!"

"Well," West says. "I gotta go. He's wild, Nolan. Count yourself lucky to have that sweet baby girl. Boys, man. High insurance rates, drunken games of beer pong, and sports doctors are all I see in my future. I hope I have a girl next. I already know how to throw a football. I'd like to learn how to throw a tea party."

And with that, he turns and jogs off after his wild kid.

Two strikes right out of the gate.

I head the other direction where I know Pax's cabaña is. But I can hear him singing an Army cadence song before I even get to the door.

"'I wanna be an Airborne Ranger! Live me a life of blood and danger!'"

I open the door and find him lying on the bed, head hanging over the edge, upside down. He smells like tequila. "Paxton?"

"'Airborne Ranger! Blood and danger!'" His eyes swing around the room as he looks for me. Then he slumps over the side of the bed and drops to the floor. "Nooooolaaaaaaaan," he croons, crawling forward. "Sing with me. 'I wanna be a scuba diver.'" He points. But I just stand there, kinda fuckin' stunned. "Sing it!" he yells.

"'I wanna be a scuba diver,'" I sing.

"'Jump right in that muddy water.'" He points to me again.

"'Jump right in—'" But then I realize he's way too drunk to look after my baby so I don't really need to play along. "Where's Cindy?" I ask. "I wanna have a date night with Ivy and I need a sitter."

"Party!" he yells. "Muddy water! Scuba diver!"

I leave. He's got issues. Obviously.

OK, so I can't ask Ellie because it might make her sad. I can't ask Victoria because she's sick. Cindy is apparently partying... so that leaves me with Katya or Rory.

I look over at the main house sitting up on a hill. It's big for an island house. Big enough for four kids and a wife? That I'm not so sure about. I'd go crazy on this island if I had to stay here all the time.

But I head up the path that leads to the house anyway. Partly because it looks inviting and friendly in the coming dusk, and partly because it's my last hope of having some alone time with Mrs. Romantic tonight.

I'm just coming around a little twist in the path when two tiny masked people jump out from the bushes and scare me half to death.

"Who goes there?" one of the little shits demands.

"Uhhh," I say. "It's me. Nolan."

"How do we know it's you?" the other tiny shit asks.

"It's me," I say. "You saw me earlier when I got off the helicopter, remember?"

"Then what are our names?" the first one asks.

Jesus. Fucking kids, right? "I can't see your faces," I say. I really don't remember. And I just want to get up to the house to ask for help, so I try to push past them.

The smaller one pokes her pointy stick into my gut and says, "I command you to stop! In the name of the queen!"

I'm getting kinda irritated now. So I say, "You guys. It's me. Nolan Delaney. I'm one of the Misters. I'm your dad's friend."

"If you're his friend, then what are our names?"

I think real hard. Five did introduce them. They aren't the twins. They're too short. So I concentrate on the smaller kids in my memory.

56

They both had long, wild, brown hair. And they both have wide brown eyes peeking through eyeholes. Which isn't helpful, I realize, because they look more alike than the damn twins. Not to mention they're wearing masks. Not ski masks. Something looser. And made of cotton. More like a hood.

"Where'd ya get those masks?" I ask, trying to change the subject. Because I have no idea what Five calls them.

"We made them," the taller one says.

"With our *hands*," the little one clarifies.

The tall one asks, "Does your wife sew, Nolan Delaney?"

"Ummm…" Does Ivy sew? "Yeah," I say. I'm pretty sure Ivy does shit like that. So my answer comes out confident.

"Do you sew?" the smaller one asks.

"No." I laugh. "I don't sew."

"Why not?" they both demand at the same time.

"I'm a dude," I say, still chuckling.

"Our daddy sews. He made us these capes."

They are some pretty nice capes. Made out of black felt. And they have some kind of logo on the back. Like superheroes or somethin'.

"And he taught us to make spears." They both shove their pointed sticks at me again.

"Ow! Jesus, you guys. I just wanna go talk to Kat and see if she'll babysit for me tonight. Can I go now?"

The taller one lifts up her black mask to show me her face. "Why do you need a babysitter?"

"Because I want to go on a date with my wife. And you're six years old, so I'm not telling you any more details."

"I'm seven," she snaps. "And you don't even know my name. Do you?"

"Maggie," I guess. I'm pretty sure it starts with M.

"Wrong," the little one says.

"Martha," I try again.

"Nope!"

"Hey," I say, kneeling down so I can look them in the eyes. "How about you tell me your names and then I'll remember them forever this time, and you guys let me go up there and ask Kat to babysit for me. Deal?"

They look at each other and laugh.

"What's so funny?"

"No deal," the older one says. "You're our prisoner now."

And then they poke me again!

"This way, prisoner," the tiny one barks. "March!"

I do as I'm told because I'm directed to march up towards the house. I figure Five will show up eventually and call off his mini-assassins, so it's easier to just go along.

But they don't lead me to the front door. They lead me around the back and stop me in front of a window.

"Look," the older ones says, pointing her stick at the window.

And that's when I get attacked by a pack of kittens.

"Ow! Motherfuckers!" I shake my leg and kittens go flying into the grass, and both of the little girls fall to their knees, giggling.

"They got you!" the tiny one exclaims.

"They got you good!" laughs the older one.

And yeah, there's blood running down my legs from a dozen kitten claw marks.

I sigh. Count to five to keep my temper under control. And say through gritted teeth, "I'm going to look for Katya now."

"She's right there," the older one says. "Look."

So I look through the window—'cause that's where her stupid pointy stick is telling me to look—and sure enough, I see both Katya and Rory in a room.

"They're putting the final touches on her wedding dress. My mommy can make dresses," the little one says.

"Pretty, pretty dresses," the taller one adds. "So she can't babysit for you."

I stare at them and throw up my hands. "Fine. I'll just go back to my bungalow and forget about date night."

"I'm Louise," the small one says.

"And I'm Mathilda," the other one says.

"Very pleased to meet you both," I say, turning to leave.

"Don't you want to ask our daddy to babysit?" Louise asks.

I stop and turn, look at them for a second and get hopeful. "Do you think he will?"

They both have another fit of giggles.

I take that as a no and turn to leave again.

"Wait!" they both say, dropping their spears and taking my hands.

"We've got plans for you, Nolan Delaney," Mathilda says.

"I don't have time. I gotta get back to—"

"You have to go to prison for trespassing," Louis says. "Thirty minutes in the gulag."

"It's the law," Mathilda says, her voice serious as all hell.

And then they push and drag me over to a small playhouse. It looks like a mini-castle and there's a light on inside.

*Just play along, Nolan,* the voice in my head says. *Go inside, stay five minutes, and then back out carefully.*

So I let them lead me towards the playhouse, thankful that they're not still poking me with those stupid pointy sticks.

Inside it looks like a princess threw up. Two princesses, really. There's a small table in the center with a tea set laid out on a white table cloth with eyelet lace edges. And each of the four small chairs has a fuzzy pink pillow on the seat.

"Sit," Louise commands.

So I sit, way too big for this chair, my knees practically touching my chin, half hoping I break the thing, half hoping I don't, since that would probably add another thirty minutes to my gulag sentence.

They pour me tea—which is water. And feed me cakes—which is crackers. And I realize I actually *am* on a date. Just not with my wife.

And that makes me smile.

They tell me stories about their life on the island. And those damn kittens find their way into my lap. And pretty soon, they pronounce me free and caution me not to break any more laws. And then I'm pushed outside the castle and told to go straight home or the king will be angry.

I wander down several pathways trying to find the one that leads back to my cabaña, wondering what the fuck just happened. Thinking maybe girls aren't that different than boys. Imagining myself with Bronte when she's that age and kinda liking that image.

Say what you want about Five and his secret island. He's got some cool kids.

I smile as I walk through the cabaña door, calling out, "Ivy?"

But she doesn't answer back. And when I wander into the bedroom, I see why.

She and Bronte are all wrapped up together. Bronte's face pressed against Ivy's breast. Ivy's fingers twined into Bronte's fine, loose curls of blonde hair.

Fast asleep.

"Fuck it," I sigh. But I'm smiling all the way through that sigh.

It wasn't the date night I imagined, but it might've been better.

I crawl into bed, Bronte between us. And if this was yesterday that might've been a bad sign. It might've meant that Bronte was an interloper. That we're kinda doomed. That things went too fast, changed too quick. That we'll never be the people we were before.

I think all those things are true now as well. But not in the bad way.

My daughter will grow up to be one of those little shits out on that path. She will poke me, and frustrate me—but she will delight me with surprises too.

I think… maybe raising a girl is gonna be a blast. And I need to learn how to do it right.

# CHAPTER TEN

# WEST

"West."

Tori is prodding me.

"What?" I mumble, still mostly asleep.

"Wake up."

"Why?"

"Ethan is gone again."

"Fuck." I lie still for a few seconds, forcing myself awake.

"I'm gonna go find him," Tori says. "You stay here."

"No," I say, pulling her back into me before she can escape. "It's an island," I say. "How much trouble can he get in on an island?"

This is something Ethan's been doing for a while now. It started a few weeks after we moved to Fort Collins and a part of me wonders if the move was too much for him. I mean, we did pull him from his life in New York— however messed up that was, it was still his life. And we moved him out to LA. Which is a culture shock all its own. And then a few months later, he was living in Fort Collins.

Colorado isn't extreme in any way. It's not New York and it's not LA, which are the two most opposite cities in the entire US. It's just a small-town place with looming mountains and unpredictable weather. It's slow, and calm, and pretty. That's it.

But he wasn't used to slow, and calm, and pretty. He was used to big, and loud, and city.

"He could drown in the ocean," Tori says.

"He's a great swimmer," I say. "He took to the ocean like he was born on Nantucket." And then I turn to her, hug her close, and say, "We could make the most of it, ya know? Have a little sexy fun?"

"Weston Conrad!"

I swing my legs out of bed, rub my hands up and down my face, and look over my shoulder at Tori. "I'll go find him."

She smiles and squeezes my hand. "I know he's fine. But he's a little boy. We can't let him keep doing this."

"I know," I say, pulling on my shorts and reaching for a t-shirt. "I get it."

Tori sighs. "I know he thinks he's big, but he's not, West. He needs to learn how to be a kid."

"I get it," I say, deciding to go barefoot. This island is filled with sand. Probably gets filled on some kind of regular basis. Because all the pathways are white, and soft, and feel very fucking good on bare feet.

I stumble out of the cabaña and look around. It's dark. I didn't catch the time, and I'm not wearing my watch, but I grew up on the ocean. And one look at the stars—one look at the Pleiades high in the southern sky—tells me it's about one AM.

I'm always the one who goes looking for Ethan at home too. I tell Tori he only goes to the porch, and most of the time he is on the porch, but I found him at City Park once. And sitting outside Shrike Bikes a second time. Both of which are about half a mile from our house.

I would've called the police both times, but then they'd start asking questions and... yeah. We don't need that.

Besides, I think I get Ethan in a way that Tori doesn't. A way that most people won't.

So I wander down towards the closest beach first, because if I was eight again, and I was on this island, that's exactly where I'd be.

I hear a weird humming sound before I get there and once I push past the final few palm fronds and the sea comes into view, I understand what it is.

Mr. Mysterious, lying down on the sand, staring up at the stars, singing some kind of army marching song under his breath.

"Hey," I say, walking over to him. "What's up?" I sink down into the sand next to him and he turns his head. Fuck, he smells like a goddamned bar.

"Drunk," he says.

"I can see that. Why are you out here on the beach?"

"I dunno," he slurs.

"Hmmm." I stare at him for a second. I don't think I know Paxton Vance all that well, but I don't think anyone really knows him. So I don't mind that too much. He's a friend. For sure. He saved my ass—and Tori's—couple times at least. So even though he's mostly an insufferable jerk, he's the kind of insufferable jerk you can't help but like.

"We're gettin' married," he says, after a long silence.

"Yup. You worried about that?" I ask.

"Are you?" he asks, turning his head towards me. But his eyes are closed. He's too fucked up to even see me shrug.

"Not really," I say. The seconds tick off and it's pretty clear he's not gonna offer up anything else. So I say, "But it's weird, right?"

"Yeah," he mumbles. "She's probably gonna hate me in like... six months."

65

"What?" I laugh. "Cindy Shrike? Dude, if ever there was a girl who could rein you in, it's her."

"I donwannabereinedin…" It comes out like one long, drunk word. And then he sings, just a little bit louder, "'I wanna be an Airborne Ranger. Live me a life of blood and danger…'"

"Ah," I say, leaning back in the sand to rest on my elbows. It makes sense now. He's Mr. fucking Mysterious. And he's about to get married. Which probably makes him think all that exciting shit he's been doing for the past— well, his whole life, I guess—is now over.

I don't really know what to tell him. Because you can't play that game forever. Not if you want a love life. I know that better than most. Hell, I might just be plain old Mr. Corporate, but my childhood was about as mysterious as it gets.

Which reminds me of why I'm here. "You seen my kid anywhere?"

He points to the ocean. "There," he says.

I squint my eyes and focus on where he's pointing.

"I'm making sure he don't drown." Pax sighs. "Just being a good friend."

Which makes me laugh. Like a real, honest-to-goodness laugh. "I don't know if you're really qualified to play lifeguard. But what the fuck is he doing?"

Ethan is nothing but a black silhouette against a gray night sky lit up by a rising moon. He's standing on a rock, waves crashing all around him, one arm drawn back.

"Spearfishing," Pax says, opening his eyes to look at me. Like that explains everything. "He came up. Asked me if I had a knife."

"Why?"

"To make a fucking spear," Pax growls. "So I gave him my knife."

"OK," I say, like this is all just normal shit for a Mister kid. Because it is. Ethan's got some kind of story to tell, I'm just not sure he's ever gonna tell it. "I guess I better go get him."

"Prolly," Pax says, eyes closed again. "I can't watch everybody, Weston Conrad. I can't. Not if I wanna be happy."

And that explains everything too.

So I say, "You've been relived of duty, soldier." And then I slap him on the stomach, which makes him groan and push me away. I stand up so I can look down at him. "Find another army to work for. This one doesn't need you anymore."

I walk out to the beach, swim over to the rock outcropping Ethan is standing on, and pull myself up, dripping wet.

It feels like coming home for some reason.

"Hey," Ethan says, just before he throws his spear.

"Hey," I say, watching it hit the target below the surface of the water.

Ethan jumps into the ocean. Fearless. Determined. He grabs his spear, and then hoists himself, and his catch, back up onto the rocks. He slides the fish off the end of the stick and it plops down into his pile.

He's got... one, two, three, four... ten. Ten fucking fish on this pile of rocks.

"Looks like you've caught your quota," I say.

He stares at me for a second, squinting in the bright moonlight, then looks at his catch and seems to do a mental calculation. "Do you think it's enough?"

"For what?" I ask, genuinely curious.

"Breakfast," he says. Like this is obvious.

"I'm pretty sure Five and Rory have enough food for everyone. We don't need to provide it."

"I know," Ethan says. And for an eight-year-old, he sure does come across like he's walked this earth forever.

"So we're good?" I ask. "We can go to bed now?"

He stares up at me like he really wants to say no. But then he looks out at the beach where Pax is still singing his Airborne Ranger song and says, "OK. But we can come back tomorrow, right?"

"Sure," I say. "Sure. I'll bring you back tomorrow to fish."

Ethan nods at me and then produces a fishing line, hooks all his fish onto it, and hoists it over his shoulder. "Cool," he says, jumping back into the water.

We swim back, drag ourselves out of the ocean, and head towards the bungalows.

"How old were you?" he asks.

"When?" I ask.

"When you had to fish for a living."

"Older than you," I say. Which is a lie. I was his age exactly. But I don't want him to know too much about who I was back then.

"How much older?" Ethan persists.

"A few years."

"And that's when you found that gold?"

Shit. "Where'd you hear about that?"

"I heard Oliver talking to Katya a while back."

I search my memory for when he'd have that opportunity and come up blank.

"I snuck out," Ethan says, like he's reading my mind. "And I was over at Oliver's house."

Oliver lives down the street from Shrike Bikes. And suddenly I realize, I have no idea what my son does at night. "Did they know you were there?" I ask.

"Nope," he says through a smile. "I'm sneaky when I wanna be."

"Very." I laugh. "But it's late, Ethan. And I need to think about this for a little bit before we talk anymore. So do you think—for your mother's sake—you can stop being sneaky until we have that talk?"

"Why?" he asks.

"Because she's worried about you."

He stops walking. Which makes me stop walking. And he says, "Are you worried about me?"

My entire childhood flashes before my eyes as I think about his question. All the things I did. The people I was around. The danger, and the excitement, and the mystery.

And I decide… "No. No, I'm not that worried, Ethan."

"Good," he says, starting to walk again. "Because I can take care of myself. I like you guys, so I stick around. But I don't need you guys."

I watch him go. Just stand there on the path and watch him go. He disappears through the jungle of palm trees and tropical ferns.

"Yeah," Pax says, stumbling up to me. "He's here because he wants to be. And there's nothing you can do to change that, West." And then it's his turn to slap me in the gut. "Because that kid is just like us. We were born this way. This is just who we are. And putting him in a pretty house, on a peaceful street, and giving him parents can't change that."

I watch him disappear through the trees too. Wondering if there's any hope for us at all. Have we been through too much? Did we fuck it all up years ago and there's no going back?

I mean, look at us. Even perfect Mr. Perfect is struggling with normal life. Nolan is in way over his head with that baby girl, everyone can see it. I've adopted a kid who's lived through something big, and he's never gonna forget it. Mysterious is already missing his old life and the new one hasn't even started. And Match… Match is trying to pretend nothing's happening. Nothing to see here. Everything's great.

But it's all an illusion, isn't it?

Just one. Big. Fat. Lie.

CHAPTER ELEVEN

# PAX

I don't know how long I wandered the jungle after I left West and the kid, but I do know I passed out. And when I finally open my eyes again and figure out I'm on the beach again, I start humming I Wanna Be an Airborne Ranger.

"'Live me a life of blood and danger.'"

I turn my head and realize Cindy is next to me. The sand is cold, so I absently wonder if she's cold. "Hey," I say. My voice is all raspy and my head is still kinda spinning.

"'I wanna be a scuba diver,'" she sings. Softly. Not the way it's supposed to be—all loud and chanty for marching.

"'Jump right in that muddy water,'" I say.

"'Scuba diver,'" she whispers, placing her head on my chest. Like she wants to make sure I'm still here. That my heart is still beating.

"'Muddy water,'" I reply.

"'I wanna be a paramedic,'" she continues.

"'Shoot some blissful anesthetic.'"

"'Airborne Ranger.'"

"'Muddy water.'"

"'Anesthetic.'"

"It's not what you think," I say, ending the song.

"I don't think anything, Detective. I'm just here, ya know?"

"I'm not having second thoughts," I say, wanting to make this clear. "Not about you, anyway."

She props herself up on her elbow and stares at me. The moon is setting, but it's enough light to see the blue of her eyes. "Then what's going on?"

"I did something," I say. "Something…"

She swallows hard. "Something you need to talk to me about?" she asks, her voice shaking slightly.

I nod my head.

"So talk."

I take a deep breath and let it out. Try and think of where to begin. But… it's all pretty fucked up. So I turn my head and stare up at the stars.

"I was with Rory tonight," Cindy says, changing the subject.

I look at her again. Study her. I don't deserve this woman. Not at all. "How'd it go?"

"Good," Cindy says, lying back down in the sand. She puts her hands behind her head and just stares up at the dark sky. "She's like…" And then she laughs. "She's just like my mom. It's so weird. I mean, I never thought of her as a sister. Not really. We're so far apart in age, ya know?"

But I don't know. I don't have any siblings. I have almost no family at all. Just my mom, who is very cool as far as moms go. Maybe not as kickass as Veronica Shrike, but still. I love my mom. And she can hold her own as far as I'm concerned.

"I was gonna watch a movie the other day," Cindy says, changing the subject again. She looks at me. We stare at each other. "But there was already a movie in the Blu-ray."

I wince.

"It was Challenge Accepted."

"Yeah," I say. "I was watching it a couple weeks ago. I guess I forgot to put it back."

"Charles was pretty good in that movie. I watched it. Just curious, ya know. I was trying to see if you looked like him."

"Do I?" I ask.

"Yeah," she says. "Like... kinda a lot. It's weird. You look like a movie star, Pax."

"Well." I laugh. "Then I guess it's a good thing you look like a starlet, Miss Cookie. We're perfect for each other."

"Destined to be together," she adds.

"Destined," I say. "For sure."

"Do you want to stay out here on the beach? Or do you want to come to bed with me?"

I smile. "Bed."

"Then let's go." She stands up, grabs my hand, and then pulls. I'm still a little bit drunk, so it takes me a second, but I get it together and don't lean on her too much as we find our way back to the bungalow.

When we get inside we leave the lights off. She lifts up my shirt and I help her get it over my head. Then she unbuckles my shorts and pulls them down.

I just stare at her. Wondering what she's thinking right now.

She bites her lip and I want to kiss it. I want her to stop thinking. I want to take her to bed and hold her tight, and just forget what I did.

I wait for the question to come again. But it doesn't. She just sighs as she takes off her shirt. She's got no bra on. Like she was in bed before she came looking for me. And then she wiggles her shorts over her hips, lets them drop to the floor and takes my hand again. She leads me to the bed, and we get in, cover up with the soft covers, and hug each other. Hold each other close.

I wonder how she got so patient. Because she's very patient with me. We've done some crazy shit over the past year. We started our own investigation business and we've made a pretty good go at it. We mostly stay in Fort Collins to be near my friends—who are now her friends—and her family, who are now my family, but we travel a lot. Mostly to Southern California, since that's where most of my clients are. I don't fix things for people anymore.

Usually.

But I'm in the middle of some fixing right now and that's what's eating me up.

So I say, "I'm doing something." But then I don't know how to continue and just let that bullshit hang there.

"OK," she says.

"And I don't want to talk about it yet."

"All right."

"But I love you."

"I love you too. That's why I'm marrying you, Detective."

"It's gonna be a great wedding," I say, then realize... it might not be.

But she says, "I know. I'm not worried about the wedding. I don't even care about the wedding. I just like being here with everyone else, ya know? And you. I like the islands. I don't think we spend enough time on the islands."

"I love it here," I say. "Hey, you know what Nolan told me tonight?"

"What?"

"He was looking for a babysitter so he could take Ivy out on a date."

"Did he find one?"

"No idea. But I like the thought of a date with you, Miss Cookie."

She snort-laughs. "Yeah?"

"Yeah, so let's make our last day together as single people a date day. What do ya say?"

"One last date before we're married? You're building up some high expectations in me, Detective."

I laugh... but she's right.

"What will we do?" she asks.

"We could..." I start thinking up ways to impress Cinderella Shrike. Something spectacular. And fun. And sexy. And that we can do on an island. Scuba diving, snorkeling, surfing—not that this place is really surfable, but we could try. Or maybe build a sand castle, or have a picnic, or hike around the island. Maybe there's a cave. We like spelunking.

But we've done it all. Our lives this past year have been exciting and fun. Pretty much one hundred percent of the time.

"You know what?" Cindy says, reaching down to grab my dick.

"What?" I say, turning into her so I can kiss the soft skin of her breasts.

"Leave it to me. You've got something on your mind, so let me take care of it."

I wait to see if she's gonna ask me more. If she wants to know what I'm up to. What's got me so worried. Is she picturing me getting caught? On trial for any of the nefarious things I've done in the past? Serving time? Leaving her alone... adrift... lonely?

"OK?" she asks in my silence.

"OK," I say, bringing my kiss up to her lips.

I just want to enjoy her. Forever.

But forever is a myth. I think everyone knows that. In the back of their heads, right? There's no such thing as forever. So weddings... that whole eternity thing.

It's bugging me.

# CHAPTER TWELVE

# OLLIE

"Hey," I call out to Cindy the next morning as Kat opens the bungalow door and waves her inside. "Where's Pax?"

"Sleeping off a wicked hangover after getting drunk all by himself last night."

Katya and I both exchange raised eyebrows.

"What's that all about?" I ask.

Cindy sighs and then slumps down into a chair.

"He does drink a lot," Kat says.

Which I cannot argue with. Fucking Mysterious has been known to drink before noon plenty of days. But he doesn't often go on binges. It's usually just a glass of Scotch when things blow up. He likes to pour them and then not finish them too. I think it's a habit. Like... the act of handling that crystal decanter and the clink of the ice just kinda sets his world right so he can think straight.

"He's not an alcoholic," I say, shooting Katya a look.

She shoots one back. "I didn't say that."

"I know he's not an alcoholic, you guys," Cindy says. "I've lived with him for a year now. Which is why last night kinda worries me. You're right, Ollie. He doesn't go on binges unless shit is really wrong."

"So what's wrong with him?" I ask. Now it's Katya's turn to shoot me a look. "What?" I ask.

"I'm still trying to figure it out. We're going on a date today."

"That sounds fun," Kat says, folding her legs underneath her as she relaxes on the couch. "What are you guys gonna do?"

"I don't know yet. It was his idea, but then he looked really worried that he might not come up with something worthy of the day before our wedding. So I told him I'd do it."

I say, "You should hang out with all of us."

"No," Kat says. "They want to be alone, Oliver. Not hang out with a bunch of people."

"Yeah, which is why I suggested it. I still can't picture my little sister with my best friend."

"I'll think of something," Cindy says. "If there's one thing I've got going for me, it's my bountiful imagination."

"I'm pretty sure Mysterious is far more interested in your bountiful other things."

They both shoot me a look.

Then Cindy stands up and says, "You guys should go on a date too." But she's talking to Katya, not me. "Keep my brother out of my business. Because I might punch him if he doesn't get over this stupid little sister bullshit."

"You're the one who came over here," I shout. But she's already gone.

"What is your problem?" Kat asks.

"My problem is that my best friend stole my baby sister."

"Stole her, Oliver? Really? Stole her?"

"Yeah," I say. "Like how is this rocket science? I got one little sister, Kat. One. And he took her. It's not right."

"She tricked him."

"She was practically a baby when that happened."

"It was last year."

"Exactly my point! Besides, he's Mr. fucking Mysterious. He can't figure out the jailbait girl at his front door bringing him sandwiches—who looks exactly like my mom, by the way!—is off limits?"

Katya just laughs at me. "You're being ridiculous."

"I'm being...? No. He stole my sister."

She scrunches her eyebrows up at me. Opens her mouth. Pauses. Then says, "You're not mad at Five. And if you ask me, he did a lot worse than sweep your sister off her feet."

"Five's different," I say. "I mean, come on. He's Five."

"So? Pax is one of your oldest friends. He's saved your ass, right? He'd do anything for you. You've barely seen Five, yet you make all the excuses for him."

"Five and Rory... well, it's just different, Kat. You don't understand."

"Then explain it to me."

"They're like... soulmates. They've known each other since birth. Rory belonged to Five before I was even born. It's... it's just different."

"OK," she says. "But you know what?"

"What?" I ask, tired of this conversation.

"I have no family, Oliver." I look over at her. Suddenly feeling stupid. "No one but you. I have no parents, my sister is dead, everything is gone."

"I didn't mean it... I mean... I'm sorry, Kat."

"Don't be sorry for me. I have so much more now that I became part of your world. And I consider Pax a friend. More than just a friend. He's like a brother now. And Mac too. And Nolan, and West. They're the brothers I never had. And I think we both know that if I was in trouble and you weren't around, I could go to them—any of them—

and they'd take care of me. But you know exactly who I'd go to first, right?"

I roll my eyes.

"Say it," she says. "Because you need to stop this stupidity and admit what you won't."

"Fine," I say. "You'd go to Pax. He'd take care of everything like it never happened. You'd never get caught. I should be happy he's the one taking care of my sister. I should get over it and wish them well, etc, etc, etc."

She just does one of those little huffs. Like a laugh, but not a laugh.

"What now?"

"You really can't see what you're doing?"

"What am I doing?"

She crawls across the couch and places herself in my lap, both hands on my cheeks as she stares down at me. She kisses me. Just a small kiss. But she's smiling as she does it. I can feel her grin.

"You're being you, I guess."

I think about that for a second. "You make that sound like a bad thing."

"Nope," Kat whispers, still kissing me. But then she sighs and drops her head to my chest. "Your sister—not Cindy, Rory—she's amazing."

"Yeah," I say. Even though I barely know her. What I know of Rory is mostly based on memory. And those memories are mostly that summer Five came home. And I tricked her, and I tricked him, and things were good, and the days were long, and hot, and perfect.

"Cindy and I tried on our dresses last night."

"Yeah?" I ask. I cannot fucking wait to see Katya in her dress. I'm really looking forward to this wedding. Not just for us—even though I think we need this milestone—but the whole thing. All the guys and all their girls. And Five is gonna marry Rory for real. It's just… kinda great.

"And Cindy said she was having second thoughts about her dress. That it was too risqué, and showed too much leg. But I said, 'That's just you, right? So why not be you on your special day?' And Cindy said, 'Yeah. You're right. Maybe it needs to be even sexier?'"

"Jesus…" I moan.

"So Rory says, 'I can alter it if you want. Make it your dream dress.'"

"God, she's just like my mom." I like hearing this stuff about Rory.

"So she does that. She adds some lace and cuts a slit, and starts sewing. And then Rory looks at me and says, 'Is this your dream dress, Kat?' I like how she calls me Kat and not Katya. Like we're already old friends. So I say, 'Yeah. Pretty much.' I feel like I tried on hundreds of dresses and every time I thought one was better than the rest. It was almost too much, ya know? And now I think maybe I made a mistake. So Rory says, 'What would you do different?' So I say… 'I'd maybe like it to be a little more traditional. You know, like glass beads and shit.'"

I'm transfixed as I picture the whole scene.

"So Rory says, 'I have some glass beads. Should I sew them onto your bodice?' And I say, 'Yeah, do it.' So she does. Well, she's doing it today or did it last night, or whatever. All I know is that it's special, right? That your sister is adding to my dress. I love it actually. Because I love her. I love all of them. Even bitchy Ariel."

I snort-laugh at that.

"I feel like… I'm gaining so much, ya know? Even though I'm still pretty new and your mom looks at me funny sometimes, I think one day it'll all be normal."

I hug her close. Hold her tight. Kiss her neck. "I'm sorry your family is gone. But Mariel will be here too."

"I know." She smiles. "I know. I love Mariel."

And I suddenly get it. "And you love Pax because of Mariel," I say.

She nods. "I think so. He's nice to me. So it's like... he's family in all the ways, Oliver. You're lucky to have so much family. You should enjoy him. And he and Cindy are perfect for each other. Leave them alone. Be supportive. It's not really him you're mad at anyway."

Then she gets up and says, "I'm taking a shower. Come fuck me against the wall."

I laugh. And follow her in. And I do fuck her against the wall.

But then later, when I'm holding her hand and we're walking up to Rory's house to find some breakfast, I wonder what she meant about that statement.

Who does she think I'm really mad at?

CHAPTER THIRTEEN

# FIVE

I'm outnumbered. That's the thing when you live on an island with nothing but females. Well, mostly females. We have a cook who's a guy. And the helicopter pilot, he's a guy. And we used to have a horse trainer who was a guy. But he's been gone for a while now and the cook doesn't even talk to me because I'm kind of a picky eater, and the pilot is, well, only here to fly the fucking helicopter, and helicopters aren't really conducive for complaining about your wife and daughters ganging up on you.

So it's just me and them.

And right now, they're all glaring at me. Even Louise is against me. Sweet, tiny, five-year-old Louise stomps her foot and says, "I wanna go to school too!"

Jesus.

"You're not part of this conversation." I say, pointing my finger at her. She stomps her foot again, crosses her arms in defiance, and then pouts her lips. "Go play," I say, pointing to her and Mathilda. They both hesitate, wondering how far they should push this. But I make dad eyes at them and that's all it takes.

They sulk off, complaining the whole time.

I take my attention back to Ellie, Ming, Rory, Ana, and Isa. Five fucking girls. All of them against me.

"Listen," I say, switching into my reasonable voice.

"No, you listen," Rory says. "Ming is here, we've been planning this for months, and the girls want to take the test. Don't you, girls?"

There is a chorus of, "Yes, Daddy! We do!" And I wonder if they plan that twin shit, or if they make that harmony just on instinct? I should ask my brother and sister. They're twins too.

"You're not gonna win," Mac says from the kitchen. He's leaning against the countertop eating a bowl of cereal, acting like this is no big deal. "Just let them take the test. What can it hurt?"

What can it hurt? I sigh. It can ruin everything. All the planning and shit we've been doing for… well, half our lifetimes, it seems now.

"It's not far from us," Mac continues. "We'll keep an eye on them."

I shoot Rory a look. Because there's no way she's gonna let her little girls go off to boarding school. No way. If they go, we all go. And this island life will be over.

I run my fingers through my hair and turn to look out the window. Take it all in. Already missing it.

"Fine," I whisper.

And the entire room erupts in cheers.

I don't cheer. Or feel happy. In fact, I think I'm the only one on this island who thinks today is the worst day ever.

"Let's go, girls," Ming says. "I'm ready when you are."

It's a long test. Like four parts to it or something like that. I took it once. A long time ago in some other life I barely remember.

I turn to watch them disappear out the door. Rory and Ellie set up the palapa near the pool for testing. I guess, if you gotta take an all-day test, this isn't a bad way to do it.

"Don't be mad at me," Rory says, grabbing hold of my arm and tugging me towards her.

But I am kinda mad. "You should've talked to me about it first."

"You would've said no," Rory says.

"Which should've been your first clue that this wasn't a decision you can just make on your own."

"I get a say, Five Aston. After all these years of doing what you think is best, it's my turn to take the reins. And it's your turn to listen."

I don't want to fight with her. We're not that kind of couple. We don't normally have much to argue about.

But then there's this little voice in my head that's telling me, That's because she gives in to you, Five. And you let her.

"This is gonna be good for us, Five," Rory insists.

But I just don't agree. And she knows me well enough to see that written all over my face. I just don't agree.

She walks off, disappearing outside with the girls.

"You don't want to fuck this up," Mac says, still slurping his cereal.

"No," I say, turning to face him. "Fucking this up is the only thing left to do. I need you to steal those tests, Perfect. Maybe we can replace them with altered tests? Like… make sure the girls fail. Yeah, that's a great idea."

"That's the dumbest idea I've ever heard. Are you listening to yourself? Or them? Your family is sick of this place, Five. Paradise isn't paradise when it's nothing but a prison. There's a whole world out there and your family needs to see it."

"The whole world is gunning for us, Mac! How do you—of all people—not see that?"

"Maybe that was true once," he says, coming towards me, his flip-flops snapping on his feet as he walks. "But hell, even if they were coming, we know their game now. We're ready for it. And you can just move to Colorado with them. Make them live at home with you. That's what I'd do."

"Colorado?" I just stare at him, speechless. "The worst—absolute fucking worst—place they could go. If they're looking for us, that's where they'll look first!"

"You're paranoid, ya know that?"

"Fuck you."

"And stupid," he says, walking over to the door, like he's done with me. "Because Colorado is the safest place on Earth. Everyone is already there. Me, Nolan and Ivy, West and Tori, Pax and Cindy, Oliver and Katya. Not to mention your psycho father, and those crazy Shrike sisters. Hell, Spencer Shrike scares the shit out of me, man. And Veronica's brothers..." He shakes his head. "Dude," he says, throwing up his hands. "Colorado is filled with some of the most dangerous people ever. And they all seem to be related to you in some way. You've practically got an army there. What the fuck more do you need?"

I try to think real fast. Try to come up with some salient point that will sway everyone back to my side, but Mac makes it to the door and leaves before I come up with it.

"James!" I yell after him. "James Fenici would never do this!"

James Fenici knows what's up. He's kept his family secluded on an island for longer than me. And he's the best. The motherfucking best.

"I'm doing my best!" I yell.

But there's no one left to hear me. No one cares what I think. They want their freedom. Fuck safety. Fuck all my best-laid plans. Fuck paradise. My kids want school, and friends, and parties, and dances, and dresses, and boyfriends.

And my wife wants…

What does Rory want out of this? More friends? Access to stores? A river in the back yard instead of an ocean?

But it's not any of those things and I know it.

My queen wants her family back. Our small unit just isn't enough anymore.

# CHAPTER FOURTEEN

# MAC

I can sorta see Five's point. Sorta. But he's Five fucking Aston. He's got so much going for him. And yeah, that's not a guarantee, but there's no such thing as a guarantee in life. At the very least he's got the odds stacked in his favor.

I should probably be more worried than I am. I don't have shit compared to him. Well, except the other Misters. I think Mysterious and Match make up for most of what I'm lacking. And I'd never count Corporate out when it comes to sneaky plans. Dude had that secret his whole life and never told anyone. It's impressive. Not to mention Tori. Jesus. And Katya. And Cindy. Plus, Nolan can fly a plane and a helicopter. And he's rich as fuck. He's got way more money than I do these days, so we have no shortage of funding.

Nope. I'm not gonna worry about shit unless I have to, and so far I see no evidence that we're still in danger. I'm not blind. I know that the security I feel today can turn into imminent danger tomorrow, but why worry about tomorrow when today is all you got?

"You're not gonna stay here, are you?" I ask Ellie as I walk up to the table under the palapa. Ellie is out by the pool with Ming, Rory, and the girls. Cindy is here now too. Busy talking to her newly acquired nieces.

"Nah," Ellie says, sliding her arm behind my back and hooking a finger into the belt loop of my cargo shorts. "I hear today is date day."

"Is it?" I chuckle.

"Yes. Cindy just said so."

"What'd I say?" she asks, coming towards us.

"It's date day, right?"

She frowns and looks up at me. "Yeah. We wanna have a date day. But I'm in charge of the date planning since Pax is all fucking morose and shit, and I don't know what to do."

"Why's he morose?" I ask. Morose isn't a word I'd normally use to describe Mr. Mysterious.

Cindy blows out a long sigh. "I think he's worried about getting married."

I squint my eyes at her. "Worried how?"

"He's been singing this stupid song since yesterday. He was even humming it in his sleep."

"What song?" I ask.

"*I Wanna Be an Airborne Ranger.*" She sings out the title and I recognize it immediately from some movie I saw as a kid.

"Hmm…" I say.

"Yeah." She huffs. "He's already missing his life of blood and danger. How can marriage compete with that?"

"I don't think that's it," Ellie says.

"No?" Cindy says. "Well, I do. Which means I need a really good idea for date day. Help me!"

"You should do what Mac did to win me over," Ellie says.

"What'd I do?" I ask.

Ellie shoots me an annoyed look. "The scavenger hunt?"

"Oh, yeah." I laugh. "That was pretty fucking cool."

"Scavenger hunt…" Cindy thinks this over for a few seconds. "That sounds fun. Tell me all about it."

So Ellie starts talking and we relive the night together—leaving out most of the sexy stuff—as Cindy listens.

Date day, huh? Not a bad idea. I mean, Ellie has been down about this baby stuff. I should make her forget about it by planning a date day. So I say, "Hey, I'll catch up with you later," and then leave to go find Nolan. He is, after all. Mr. fucking Romantic. He'll have a good idea about what makes a good date day.

I turn a corner on a jungle path and practically bump into him. "Hey," I say. "Where you going?"

"Up to Five's house." He eyes me for a second.

I wait for him to add to that, but he doesn't, so I say, "Why?"

"Just… just… no reason."

OK. Whatever. Romantic can keep his damn secrets. "Well, I need some advice."

"'Bout what?" he asks, looking past me, down the path.

"Date day. Apparently Cindy is doing this date day thing—"

"That was my fucking idea," he interjects.

"Well, that makes sense. And thank you, because it seems to have caught on and I'm doing it too. Which is why I was looking for you. I need a good date day, dude. Something that will make Ellie forget about not being pregnant."

He scrubs a hand down his face as he thinks. "Just go the dirty sex route," he finally says. "I gotta go."

And then he's off.

JA HUSS

Fucker.

Dirty sex route. I dunno. I mean, I'm pretty good at the dirty sex stuff. Well… the fun kind, at least. But I could've used a little fucking guidance, ya know?

Fucker.

And now I'm pissed that Cindy is taking my scavenger hunt idea. Because that was goddamned clever. And I really need a clever idea.

This is the day before our wedding. I need to show Ellie how much I love her. My idea needs to be original and fun. Romantic and sexy. It needs to be everything. Just like that night we fell in love.

I need surprises. But how do you surprise someone you've shown all your secrets to? We own a helicopter, so I can't even pretend that a helicopter ride around the Caribbean would work. We've been on a boat, we've been scuba diving, and there's no way in hell I can make a picnic on the beach good enough to wow the woman I love.

Just then Corporate appears on a path up ahead, crossing the path I'm already on. "Hey!" I call out.

He turns, frowns, and then says, "What's up?"

"I need an idea, dude. For a date day."

"Date day. You're doing that too? Seems to be the thing to do today."

"I need something good, West. What can I do on this island?"

"You can take my boat if you want."

"Where to?" I ask. "I mean, where the fuck is there to go?"

He thinks for a second. Like maybe he's picturing the sea in his head trying to come up with a destination. "There's an island about ten miles west of here. They have caves there."

92

"How do you know that?" I ask.

"It's my fucking job to know that. So I checked the whole area out before we came. You can take her into that cave. There might be tourists there, though. Ethan loved it when we stopped on the way here. Had the time of his life scrambling around exploring."

"Hmmm..." I say, thinking. "I dunno. Sounds kinda dangerous."

Corporate snort-laughs. "OK, well, I gotta ago. I'm thinking up my own date day."

"What's your idea?" I ask.

"Fuck you," he says. "I'm not telling you my amazing plan." But then he turns, reaching into his pocket, and throws me some keys.

I catch them in my hand. Stare at them for a second.

"Take the boat, Mac. Go see that island. Go walk in those caves. Or just lie on the beach and play with the pigs. And if that doesn't work, tell her something amazing. Something you'd never tell anyone else. I've got the coordinates set up in my navigation because we're gonna stop on our way home. Take her there. It's been a long time since you did something spontaneous."

He walks away.

"I'm spontaneous!" I call back. "Fuck you! I'm totally spontaneous."

"No," he yells back, already out of sight. "You're predictable."

Fuck him.

Am I predictable?

I ask myself that all the way down to the marina where I look at his boat and wonder if I should risk some time off the island. Inside I find the coordinates in the GPS system, and look at the backlit screen as it charts a course.

Ten miles. It's not so far.

I leave the boat and stand on the deck. Look up at the sky. Nothing but blue. Not a single cloud.

The ocean is pretty calm today. Almost like glass. I stare at it. Then look back at Five's island and make a promise to myself and my future wife.

# CHAPTER FIFTEEN

# NOLAN

I feel bad for cutting things short with Mac, but I'm on a mission now. A mission to be a better man. A better father. Maybe even a better everything.

"Halt!" one of the little masked miscreants yells as she jumps out of the jungle, pointing her stick at me. "Who goes there?"

"It's me," I say, annoyed. Then, "Ow, shit!" as the other little delinquent pokes me in the ribs. Didn't even see her. Fucking little villains.

"You're our prisoner!" the smaller one shouts. "March, prisoner!"

It occurs to me that it might take a little longer than I thought to warm up to them. "It's me," I say again. "Nolan Delaney."

The taller one lifts up her mask and says, "We know who you are, Mr. Romantic."

Jesus. What the fuck has Five been telling these kids? "Don't call me that, OK? I'm just Nolan now."

The taller one—Mathilda, I remember—squints her eyes. "Really?"

"Yeah, really."

"Prove it," she demands.

"How the fuck am I supposed to do that?"

The smaller one, Louise, snickers. "He said the f-word."

Mathilda pokes me again. Harder this time.

95

"Ow, dammit! Stop fucking poking me."

"You're not supposed to swear in front of children, Mr. Romantic." Mathilda sneers my name. Again.

"Yeah," Louise adds. "Mommy says it's inappropriate."

"Are you inappropriate?" Mathilda asks.

"Sorry," I say. "Just stop poking me with that stupid stick. I'm a friendly, remember? I need help."

"What kind of help?" Louise asks. She lifts her mask up now too and points her wide eyes at me.

"We don't help prisoners," Mathilda says.

"Unless you pay us." Louise laughs.

Then they're both giggling.

"OK," I say, rolling my eyes. Fucking kids. I take out my wallet and start pulling out bills. How much do kids get paid for shit these days? Five bucks? I hold out two fivers. "Here. One for each of you, how's that?"

They giggle again. "Not with money," Mathilda says.

"Yeah," Louise chirps. "We can't spend money on the island."

"Then what do ya want?"

They both look at each other. Sly grins creep up their elfish faces.

"What?" I ask, getting tired of these games real fast. "Just tell me what the hell you want."

They both poke me this time. Hard. "Jesus Christ, man! Stop that! I'm a friendly!"

Mathilda motions for Louise to follow her over behind some large palm fronds and they have a secret parley about me. There's lots of whispering and dramatic sighs.

Maybe I should just resign myself to my fate as a totally inappropriate father and go find Ivy. She's a great mother. Does Bronte really need me? I mean, really? These fucking kids are right. I'm not a role model and these thoughts about wishing for a boy just prove it. Not to mention I don't even have the good sense not to swear in front of Five's little wannabe She-Ras. I have this fucked-up reputation and one day Bronte is gonna read about me on the internet. Or worse, her friends will. And they'll be the ones to tell her who I am. What I am.

I feel sick. Because there's nothing I can do about that. Ever. I can't erase history or take back all my mistakes, or nothin'.

I am Mr. Romantic. For better or worse. Forever.

"OK," Mathilda says. "We might be able to make a deal."

"I dunno," I say, resigning myself to my fucked-up future. "This is probably stupid, anyway. Never mind. I'm never gonna turn into Mr. Respectable."

I turn to walk back to the cabaña, but Louise and Mathilda both grab my wrists and make me stop. I look down at them. I wonder if they know who their father is. Really is. But Five Aston has flown under the radar for decades. He wasn't accused of rape. He wasn't given an ironic nickname. He didn't do anything as far as the rest of the world is concerned. If anything ever leaks out and people find out about this island and his secret family he's hiding out here, he'll just be another eccentric billionaire who likes his privacy. And yeah, I read all about his father, Ford. And Rory and Cindy's father, Spencer. And even though there are a few parallels—they were accused of murder, after all, and they fucking did it—it's not the same. Being accused of rape is so much worse. Because people survive rape. They have to live with it. They remember.

No one remembers that guy they killed. No one cares because he was part of something sick and disgusting. And if they do remember anything about that whole fuck-up, it's that Ford, Spencer, and Ronin were trying to save women, not hurt them.

"What?" I ask them.

"We can help you, Nolan," Mathilda says.

"If I help you," I finish.

"Yes," Louise says.

"Well, what's the price? I might not be able to afford you."

They laugh at that. "You can," Mathilda says. "Come with us."

I follow them through the jungle for so long, I start to get paranoid. If they were a little older I might think this was a set-up. Five Aston has been one surprise after another from start to finish. Why wouldn't his children be the same way? Maybe they're gonna tie me up somewhere? Poke me with those sticks a little more? Then laugh in my face as they—

"OK," Mathilda says, halting her little three-man brigade with one raised hand. "That's what we want. If you get us that, we'll turn you into Mr. Respectable. Deal?"

I squint my eyes out at the water and see nothing but... you know, water. "You want the ocean?" I ask.

"Not the ocean, doofus," Louise quips. "Them!"

I follow her pointing finger to a few small specks on the water. Heads, I realize. Animals swimming. "What the fuck are they?"

I deserve the two sharp pokes to my ribs, but I'm about to protest anyway when Louise says, "Pigs."

"We want a pig, Romantic," Mathilda says. "A very specific pig."

"And you're gonna get him for us," Louise says.

I watch from the safety of the jungle as they swim towards the beach. Then one by one they come ashore. The first one is huge. He's got tusks and everything. I watch silently as a few more spill out of the waves after him, all of them equally as terrifying.

"Fuck that," I say. "I'm not getting you a wild pig. Your parents would kill me."

"No, not them," Louise says. "Watch."

I do that. And more pigs come out of the water. Smaller ones. Then, finally, one very tiny one.

"We want the baby pig," Mathilda says. "It's gonna die if we don't help it. It's too little."

"It's not growing," Louise adds, her voice small and sad now. "We need to save it."

"So if you get us that little pig," Mathilda says, "we'll help you."

# CHAPTER SIXTEEN

# WEST

I should be doing date day with my soon-to-be wife like Nolan, but I'm not. I'm too fucking worried about Ethan to even think about the wedding.

I just can't get that conversation out of my head. Both the one with Pax and the one with Ethan.

*I like you guys, so I stick around. But I don't need you guys. We're just born this way.*

So that's it, I guess. We're just born this way.

I love my new son. Love him. Like… he's mine now. And then I wonder if that's how my parents felt about me. Not the biological ones, they never gave a shit. Neither of them. If my mom loved me the way I love Ethan, she wouldn't have killed herself in that restaurant. I mean, I understand it's not reasonable to say she wouldn't have killed herself at all. Mental illness is overpowering in a way that renders you incapable of seeing straight. But she killed herself while I was there. While I was waiting for food in a restaurant. If she loved me—even if she couldn't control her urge to end it all—wouldn't she have made sure I didn't have to experience her final act with her?

And my father. Fuck him. Bastard.

So that leaves me with the Conrads.

"What are you thinking about?" Tori asks.

"Family," I say.

"So me and Ethan," she says.

"Yeah." I sigh. "Because that's all I've got left."

"They weren't your family, West. I don't know why you can't see this. And it would be completely normal for you to change your name back—"

"No," I say, cutting her off.

"Why? Why would you want to perpetuate the Conrad name? After everything they did to you?"

But she's missing the point. "They did a lot *for* me too, ya know."

"Like what?"

"Like got me off the fucking beach! Like fed me, like sent me to the best schools—"

"And they only did that because they knew you had the gold tucked away in some secret spot."

"They didn't need the gold, Victoria. They were fucking rich."

"Maybe," she says. "But then you should be asking yourself why they got you mixed up in all that Mister stuff in the first place."

I know why. It was because they wanted a son in the Silver Society. And the whole fucking thing is wrong. I get that too. But they're the only parents I ever really had and that has to count for something.

"Ethan already left for the beach," Tori says. "I'm gonna join him."

She turns away from me and walks down the path.

And Ethan. I mean... fucking Ethan had parents too. At one point he was part of a family. And yeah, now we're his parents, so how would I feel if he grew up to hate me? Us. Both of us. Even after we loved him, cared for him, and did all we could for him.

Even if it was all misguided.

I mean, he's gonna find out who I am eventually, right? He's gonna figure all this shit out. He's gonna know

I turned on my parents and then he's gonna wonder... will I turn on him too?

I kinda feel like... if I give up my adopted parents, that means all adopted kids feel like this. That those new parents are just the substitutes. And I don't get why Tori can't see this. She was adopted too. Her father was in some shit too. And even though he's dead and he died saving her, he got her mixed up in things. Awful things, just like my parents did. And yet we don't have this conversation, over and over and over, about *him*.

I make my way down to the beach to find them. Tori, because I love her and I know she loves me and the only reason she's so insistent on this whole Conrad thing is because she hates them. For what they did and didn't do. For the way they used me. All that shit. And Ethan, because I love that little boy. I see myself in him more and more every single day.

Which is probably the scary part.

What if he's got secrets like I did? What if... what if he betrays me, like I did my parents?

And there it is.

My problem.

I betrayed them. I fucking turned on them. They took me in, gave me a new life. A good life. No... a *great* fucking life. And yeah, it was based on something dark, and if I'm being honest, probably evil. But it was so much better than I had before.

Where would I be now if they had never shown up? Dead? In prison? Crazy, like my mom?

That day my mom killed herself in the restaurant bathroom was the worst fucking day of my life. And the day Mrs. Conrad took me in... that was the best. Never mind all the shit that came after. I felt *saved* when I became

Weston Conrad. I felt saved.

But still, it wasn't enough for me to take their side. What if... when Ethan finds out the whole truth about me he decides I'm not worthy of his loyalty either?

What if he does to me what I did to them?

Tori and Ethan are swimming out to the rock he was fishing off of last night when I reach the beach.

He's got poles—enough for all of us, because that's the kind of kid he is. And bait. He showed me this morning. Some little crabs he dug up from the sand before we even woke up. He even brought sunscreen for everyone. Because that's the kind of kid he is.

Smart. Self-sufficient. Strong.

Just like me.

One day he's gonna wake up and realize not only does he not need us, but he never loved us either. One day he's gonna walk out and never come back. Or worse, he's gonna set me up for a great big fall.

Just. Like. Me.

It breaks my heart, it really does. Because I love him. I want only the best for my first son. I want to give him the world. Every opportunity. Every advantage.

And isn't that all my parents wanted too?

And yet... it wasn't enough for me, was it?

I turned on them and Ethan will probably turn on me too. Because Tori can pretend all she wants that we're the good guys here, but no matter what Tori says, we're not. Maybe we're not the bad guys either, but we're far from perfect. We're flawed and we make mistakes. Everyone makes mistakes.

I want to forgive my mother. My dad too. But they're dead now, so that opportunity is gone forever.

"Dad!" Ethan calls from his perch on the rock.

"Come on! They're biting and I see lobsters!"

I take off my shirt as I walk across the scorching sand. I let the sun beat down on me, let the salty mist sprinkle my face as I wade into the crashing waves.

And then I go under.

The ocean covers me. Blankets me in the past. It cools me down and brings it all back.

It feels like home…

…and I remember.

I remember everything…

*I am thin. Too thin. But I'm lean too. My arms are long and my body is strong, but there's no fat on me to cushion the blows I took over the past few days and the bruises are fresh, so they are purple and crimson against my summer-tanned skin.*

*My father is dead. They told me that. So now I have no one.*

*"Hello there," the woman says. "I'm Mrs. Conrad."*

*I say nothing. Not because I'm being defiant and surly, but just because I have nothing to say. She wants something from me. I don't yet know what it is, but she wants something from me. Everyone wants something from everyone. It's just the way of the world.*

*"Are you hungry?" she asks.*

*I nod. It's just the truth. And there's no way to hide that fact because my small chest is bare like my feet, and if I were to touch my ribs, I'd feel every single one of them protrude out from my flesh.*

*"Come sit down at the table," she says. "We have plenty of food for you here. Do you like seafood?"*

*I shouldn't. Because it feels like that's the only thing I've eaten over the past few years. But I do. I love it. It makes me feel free and every time I eat the day's catch at night, I feel strong. Strong enough to go on another day. And that makes me think that if I consume what's in the sea I'll live. Even through the beatings. Even through the insults. Even through death.*

*The table is long and there's a lot of chairs. So many I feel compelled to count them. Sixteen, I come up with. But there are only three place settings. One at the very head, near the window that has an expansive view of the ocean waves crashing against rocks, and two on either side.*

*A man is sitting in the one at the head. The other two are empty now, but I know I'm supposed to sit in one and she—Mrs. Conrad—will sit in the other.*

*I take my seat and place my hands in my lap to prevent them from grabbing at the crab legs stacked on a large silver platter.*

*"You can have one, son," the man says. "Have as many as you want."*

*I catch crabs and lobsters. Almost every day in the summer. But I've never had this much food in front of me at one time.*

*"Do you like it with butter?" Mrs. Conrad asks. She recognizes the look on my face as confusion, so she adds, "Do you like to dip your crab legs in hot butter?"*

*I shrug. "I dunno," I say, in the strongest voice I can muster up through my split lips.*

*"Try it," she says, dipping some crab meat into a small dish on her plate and then putting it in her mouth. She smiles through that first taste. "Mmmm." She hums. "It's good. And it has calories you need. I don't need the extra calories." She laughs. "But you do. If you dip it in butter it will taste even better than you can imagine. And it'll make you stronger too. Help you heal," she adds.*

*I pick a crab leg from the platter and crack it near the claw, then dip the claw in the butter and suck out the meat.*

*My head swoons, that's how good the butter tastes. My whole body vibrates from the food after being starved for three days.*

*I eat. Like really eat for the first time in my life. I eat everything they put in front of me.*

*Later I get sick and throw it all up, but I don't care. Because there's a never-ending parade of food in this place they say is now my home.*

*And these people who tell me they are now my parents are going to give me everything I need. Anything I want. Forever, and ever, and ever...*

# CHAPTER SEVENTEEN

# PAX

I roll over on the bed, so fucking hot I'm sticking to the sheets. I need water.

"Water," I croak, hoping Cindy will hear me. Take pity on me. Bring me water.

But I get silence in return, so I open my eyes. Well, it's a little more complicated than that. You know when you try to open your eyes but that shit is heavy, like they're practically glued together?

I only manage to raise my eyebrows.

"Cin," I croak out again.

Silence.

"Cookie?" I sound like fucking Cookie *Monster*, that's who I sound like right now.

I roll over once more, fall off the bed, land in a tangle of sweat-soaked sheets, and give up.

I might even doze off a little, because the next thing I know, I'm being kicked and someone is saying, "Mysterious? You alive down there?"

I raise my head, manage to open one eye, and stare up at Five Aston. "Dude," I say. "I need water."

I think I say that. It mostly comes out as growls and grumbles.

But a few seconds later he sets a glass down on the floor. "What the fuck happened to you, dude?"

I don't answer, just sit up, lean against the bed, and swallow down the most delicious glass of water ever.

I hold it out when I'm done. Begging for more.

Five rolls his eyes, but takes the glass and returns with more. I gulp that too, then wipe my mouth and say, "Where's Cindy?"

"I dunno," Five says. "Haven't seen her all morning. Are you still drunk? Dude, you smell."

As with all second-day drunks, the smell eludes me. But I take his word for truth, and manage to get myself upright and on my feet. "Why are you here?" I ask, sitting back down on the bed before I fall over.

I am still drunk. How did I get so drunk?

"I need something fixed," he says, all serious and shit.

"What?" I ask.

"I said, I need—"

"No, dumbass. What do you need fixed? I can hear just fine."

He looks at me like I'm a dick. And I am. But Five Aston is too, as far as I'm concerned. We're two peas in a pod. He just hides it better.

"My kids, man—"

"You want me to off your kids? Dude—"

"Don't be a dumbass. No. I want you to steal the tests they're taking so they can't go to school next year. Or better yet," he says, getting a little more animated and excited. "No. Let the tests leave the island, then steal them. And we'll blame it on Ming." He thinks about that for a second and shakes his head. "Nah, I can't blame Ming. That will really piss the girls off. We gotta do this today."

I just look at him. "What the fuck are you talking about?"

"My kids, man! My kids are taking some school entrance exams and they're little fucking geniuses, OK?

They're gonna ace that shit. They're gonna get into the best fucking school on the planet."

"So what's the problem?" Maybe I'm too drunk to understand or maybe I'm just slow. But I have no clue where this is going.

"They can't leave the island!"

"Why?"

"Why?" he spits. "Why? You of all people know why, Mysterious. Everyone is out to get us."

I actually laugh at that.

"It's not fucking funny, OK? I've kept them safe for twelve years and now Rory is insisting that they go to school."

"Don't all kids go to school?"

"Are you a moron? Do you not speak English? They can't leave. Someone will find them, Pax. I gotta keep them here for their own safety. I can't let my little girls out in this world. It's too fucked up, man."

I rub my hand down my face. I really need a shower. "So let me get this straight… you think you can keep your kids from growing up?" I laugh. Pretty loud too.

"No," Five says. "But they're only twelve, man. Twelve!" He grabs the collar of my t-shirt and pulls me to my feet, shaking me along the way for good measure. "You're not listening to me! I need this fixed! I'm pretty sure you owe me, Mysterious. I saved your ass."

"Yeah, and got both my islands blown up with that stupid plan of yours."

"That was you, dude! That plan was yours!"

Oh, yeah, kinda was, wasn't it? "Well, fuck. I'm not sure I agree with you, bro. Kids gotta go out into the world some time, right? Just deal with it. Where the fuck is Cindy?"

Five glares at me. Like he maybe wants to punch me in the mouth right now. But he takes a deep breath and says, "Cindy's gone."

"Gone where?" I ask.

He holds up a piece of paper and it takes me a minute to realize what it is. Then I snatch it out of his hand, my heart racing like it might gallop right out of my chest… and then… and then…

And then I realize it's a joke.

Sorta.

"She left this on the bedside table. Presumably this is some kink the two of you do?"

I read the note—which is cut-out magazine letters pasted onto a piece of paper, classic kidnapper style. It says,

*Help! I'm being held prisoner in a cookie factory!*

I laugh. "Goddamned cookie factory. She's so damn cute, right?" Then I look up at Five and say, "Seriously, dude. Where is she?"

He grins. Kind of an evil grin, if I do say so.

"She ran off," he says. "That's all I know." And then he winks. Like actually fucking winks at me. "But if you help me… if you do me this favor… I'll tell you where I think she went. Because what I do know, Paxton Vance, is that she's not coming back unless you find her. Heard her tell Ellie that this morning. She's sending you on a hunt, my friend. And I also heard her say, and this is word for word, that she's gonna make you prove yourself before she shows up at that wedding."

I really am drunk right now, right? "How long was I asleep?"

"Take it or leave it, man." And then he looks at his watch. "The kids still have a few more hours of testing, so I'll give you the first hint for free. But if you cross me, Mysterious…" He makes a slicing motion across his throat. "I'll gut you."

I might actually be having a stroke. Or maybe I slept for like a hundred years, like that Rip Van Winkle dude.

"Deal?"

I sigh as I stand back up, being more careful this time so I don't wobble too much and fall over. "Whatever. You want me to fix your kids by stealing their dreams, fine. Now tell me where to find Cindy."

"Cookie factory is the clue, right?" Five says.

I look down at the note. "Guess so."

"Well, that's gotta be the kitchen house. Rory and the girls have been baking stuff for the wedding all week. Come find me this afternoon and you can pay me back then, OK?"

But before I can answer, he takes off.

"OK," I call out.

But I really need a shower, so Miss Cookie will have to wait in her bakery prison a little bit longer. Because when I find her sweet cheeks, I'm gonna spank them red for driving me crazy and then I'm gonna roll her around in sugar and lick it all off her… and I won't be smelling like yesterday's drink when I do it.


It takes me a while to find the kitchen house. Who the fuck has a kitchen house anyway? Five really needs to invest in some banging AC so he can cook in the real house, if you ask me.

But whatever. I see it up ahead now. Just a little brick building on the west side of the house. Kinda hidden by the jungle mostly, but the path leading up to it is straight, so I head that way.

I can already smell her. It's probably just the pastries and shit they're making for the wedding, but I like it. I don't call her Miss Cookie for nothin'. It smells just like her.

I try to picture what's she's got planned for me. She was all into that date day thing last night. I don't remember much about what happened yesterday beyond my fascination with *I Wanna Be an Airborne Ranger* song. But I never forget anything about my cookie, so that all came back to me.

She's probably gonna be naked. We fuck in the kitchen all the time. Once I even came home to find little chocolate chips glued all over her body with dried honey. I ate dessert first that night.

I can't really see inside, and I can't hear nothin' as I walk up to the door, either. But I can imagine it… oh, fuck, yeah.

I kick the door open like a badass and yell, "I'm here to save you, Miss Cookie!"

And get silence.

"Cookie?" I call out. "Cindy? You here?"

There's lots of flour scattered all over the place. And sugar. And now that I look closer, I see red frosting on the counter and a whole tray of cookies scattered on the floor.

I shake my head. Damn, she's good at this detective game, isn't she?

"Cin-der-ella!" I sing out. "Where are you?"

I walk around the flour-covered table and find more frosting on the floor. But... but wait.

I bend down and swipe my finger across it.

That's not frosting.

It's blood.

# CHAPTER EIGHTEEN

# OLLIE

A pack of kittens attack me just as I'm about to knock on the front door. "Fucking shit!" A few jump on my cargo shorts and start climbing up my chest.

One attacks my feet and I jump away when it bites me on the big toe, then another stands up on his hind legs and bats the air, like he's gonna take me down.

"Goddammit," Five says, opening the door. "I told those girls to keep these damn kittens out of the way." He grabs the two still clinging by one claw to my shirt, and sets them down. "You OK?"

I glance at Katya, who has her hand over her mouth, stifling a laugh. "Fine," I say.

"I don't know where Louise and Mathilda got off to this morning," Five says, "but they've been missing for about an hour now."

"Should we go look for them?" Kat asks, her face scrunched up in concern.

"Nah," Five says, waving off his worry and motioning us into the house at the same time. "It's an island." And then he smiles, like all is right with the world. "They're totally safe here. What trouble could they possibly be getting into?"

"Probably not much," I conclude. "This place is pretty amazing. I mean, shit. I wish I lived on an island like this. Would be great, huh, Kat?"

I squeeze her hand and she smiles. "I could live here," she says. "Just lie on the beach and soak up the sun all day. Of course, I'd burn like fuck. I'd have to take a boat to the nearest town regularly to buy crates of sunscreen."

"Where is the nearest town?" I ask.

"Oh," Five considers this for a moment. "Nassau is the biggest, couple hours by boat or about thirty minutes by plane. But there's a few small islands with villages between here and there we sometimes go to."

"Does Rory go?" Kat asks. "And the girls?"

"No," Five says. "They don't go anywhere local. Shit, people see Rory and the girls and they never forget them."

"Yeah," I say "My sister and nieces are pretty unforgettable."

"I can't take that chance," Five says, his voice suddenly serious.

"So where do they go?" Kat asks. "Like for a fun day out."

"Shit, Kat," I say, sensing what she's getting at. "This place is fun enough. I have so many things I want to do here, it's crazy. And you know what?" I ask her.

"What?" she says, a little bit annoyed that I didn't let Five finish.

"I think we should do them all today. That'll be our date day."

"Hell," Five says. "Is everyone doing that? Cindy has Mysterious on some crazy wild-goose chase."

"Yeah," I say. "I heard. Anyway. Tell me where to take my beautiful wife-to-be today, Five. Hit me up with all the best spots. We're gonna make the most of our last day as single people."

"You guys can take the scuba gear in the boathouse and hit the reef. It's not a huge reef, but it's cool. Lots of things to see down there."

I look at Katya to see if she's interested. "Sounds great," she says.

"Then what?" I ask. "I want to spend the entire day with her. Just the two of us."

Five thinks for a moment. "Horseback riding? We have trails all over. Or dirt bikes. Oh, hey," Five says. "We've got a speedboat on the marina too. And jet skis. You can do all that if you want. We have a second, smaller island on the east coast and it's nothing but beach, Ollie. Like, nothing but a few palm trees for shade and the best white sand you can imagine."

"Yeah, that all sounds perfect. Anything else?"

He shoots me a crooked grin and then shakes his head. "I got one other place, but I think I'll take Rory there and keep it a secret. We haven't been in a long time. If everyone else is having date day, we should too."

"Speaking of Rory," I say. "Where is she?"

"Shit." Five sighs, rubbing a hand over his face. "She's got Ming giving the twins tests today."

"What kind of tests?" Katya asks.

"Private school entrance exams," Five huffs. Like this is just pissing him off.

"What?" I ask. "You're sending the girls off to private school?"

"No," Five insists. "They're not going anywhere. Rory is crazy if she thinks I'm sending my girls off to boarding school in Colorado."

"Colorado?" I ask. "Really? That would be cool, right? They'd love it there."

119

"And we're all there," Katya adds. "That would really be great for them."

"Yeah." Five laughs. "But it's not happening. So don't get excited. Hey, I gotta go check on some shit. Just help yourself to anything you want, Ollie." He claps me on the back. "The keys to the boat and skis are down in the boathouse with the scuba gear. And the horses are in the stable. You still remember how to saddle a horse?"

"Sure," I say, smiling at Katya. I wonder if she's ever been riding before. "I wasn't into them as a kid, but I know everything there is to know about horses."

Five grins, probably thinking about how Rory used to ride and show horses when they were kids. "And grab some food from the kitchen. We've got all kinds of shit in there. Take some with you. Have a picnic on the beach."

And then he leaves us there to sort things out.

"So what first?" I ask Kat. "Scuba diving? Dirt bikes? Horse back riding? Or boating?"

"Let's start with the dirt bikes," Kat says, her face flushed with excitement. "I've never ridden one before. Then we can get on the horses and ride them down to the beach, grab the scuba gear, and then end the day with a picnic on the sandy island."

"Perfect," I say, leaning down to kiss her. I just want her to be happy and forget the fact that she's got no family left. Well, that's not true. She's got me and I've got a huge family. Plus Mariel and Pax. And all the girls.

I know we can't replace her sister and parents, but we can come in a close second best if I set things up right. So that's what I'm gonna do. Not make her forget her past, but replace it with something better. "Hey," I say, my chest filling with love for this girl who decided to turn my world upside down. "I have a better idea…"

I pull her close, my hand slipping up inside her tank top.

"Not here." She giggles.

"Then where?" I ask. "Back at the bungalow?"

"No," she says, still laughing. "I'm not a prude, Mr. Match." Which makes me laugh, because no. She is most definitely not a prude. "I don't need to be under the covers in the dark. We can do it anywhere but in your brother-in-law's house. How's that?"

"Deal," I say, kissing her neck. "Then we're gonna do it all over this island today. And what better way to start the day than with sex on a bike?"

"That's a promise I'm gonna make you keep," she coos back, turning in my arms so she can kiss my chin. Her blue eyes stare up at me with… trust.

And I believe in that trust. I think I can make her happy. Give her the best life. A life she never had before me. Ease the pain of losing everything and give her something brand new. "I'll pack up breakfast and then we'll grab some real shoes from the house and see this island the way it's supposed to be seen. Every inch of it. Together."

# CHAPTER NINETEEN

# FIVE

I'm peeking out from behind a palm frond to assess the situation on the pool deck. Rory is standing off to the side, biting her nails. Like she's nervous our babies might fail.

Shit, if I was worried about that I'd be all set. None of this sneaking around would be necessary. But there's no way our babies will fail this test. Gonna ace it for sure. Gonna get into any goddamned school they want, no doubt. Gonna wanna move away and never come back.

And for a moment, it's not the idea of them getting hurt that bothers me. It's the never coming back part... by choice.

What if they go out there and fall in love with it? Make all kinds of new friends and Jesus, soon they'll be wanting boyfriends and then jobs, and then college, and marriage and...

Fuck that.

I can't deal. They're just babies. My little princesses. How in the world did Spencer Shrike ever let his girls grow up? I can't imagine it. Not even a little bit.

I look at Rory and realize she is the spitting image of her mother when she was younger. Bombshells, both of them.

And then I glance at my two girls sitting under the palapa, pencils in hand, furiously writing... and understand what growing up really means.

They will be bombshells too. They will be beautiful, and alluring, and men will fall in love with them—the same way Spencer fell in love with Veronica and I fell in love with Rory.

But it's different. I'm my father's son. Which means I'm one of us. Who will they fall in love with who can protect them the way I can? Who?

There isn't a single worthy man on this planet, let alone two of them. And then I wonder the same thing about Louise and Mathilda. Jesus Christ, what was I thinking bringing four princesses into this fucked-up world?

I need to stop this before it starts. I don't know what kind of future I want for them other then to be safe. And for as long as they've been alive, this place—this island—it's been our haven. Our sanctuary. Our refuge. An oasis in the middle of turbulent global politics, and secret shadow governments, and assassins who don't have a name, but a number.

I need to convince Rory, that's what I need to do. I'm almost sure Mysterious is gonna fuck up this job. He's a mess about something. Probably afraid to get married and give up his exciting life as mastermind fixer.

I almost laugh at that. Because Oliver is not happy about that little match-up at all. If the Vance-Shrike wedding falls apart before tomorrow he'll probably celebrate.

Point is, I can't trust Paxton to get the job done. I need to go right to the woman in charge herself.

My wife.

An evil Five Aston plan creeps into my mind. Date day. My wife, who is still worriedly looking at our twins as they test as she bites her nails, just needs to be reminded that I know best.

And I do.

But I need to get her alone.

So I creep around the edge of the pool deck, being careful to stay hidden in the palm fronds, and when I'm right behind her I stalk up, wrap my hand around her face, cup it tight over her mouth and say, "Come with me, queen. We've got a date planned."

I take her hand and lead her away. She's still looking over her shoulder at the girls, but I tug a little and she turns back to me and smiles. "Where are we going?"

"You'll see…"

We haven't been up this path in a long time. Maybe almost a year. Which makes me sad. Because we used to come up here at least once a week when we were younger. Before kids, and kitchen houses. When all we had was a little three-room house that wasn't even close to the palace I imagined giving her all growing up.

But Rory never complained. Ever. She loved our little house. And it's still standing. We mostly use it for storage now. But it was our only home for several years while the main house and out buildings were being built. It took forever to get this island to the way it is now. Almost ten years because we did everything in stages and had to hire out locals from Nassau, transport them here, put them up in makeshift tent homes, and yeah… fucking hassle.

She was a trooper through all of it.

"I love you," I say, looking over at her.

"I love you too," she says, smiling back at me.

"No," I say. "I mean… you're everything to me, Rory. You and the girls. You're all I ever wanted or needed." I stop on the path, take her face in my hands, and kiss her.

Long. Soft. Our tongues doing that little dance we've perfected over the years. "I love you." I whisper it this time.

"We're not people," she says, talking right into my mouth. Her words flirting with my tongue. "We're made of moonlight, and twinkling stars, and the night."

I laugh, remembering the night I told her that. Just a small, sad laugh. "We're perfectly matched. Your blue eyes."

"And your brown ones," she says, finishing the promise we made to each other so long ago. "We're soulmates, Five Aston."

"We are, Rory Aston."

She smiles big when I call her that. She's not legally Mrs. Aston, but she's always been mine, so that's legal enough for me.

"Come on," I say, reluctantly pulling away. "We've got a date with paradise."

She knows where we're going. This path only leads one place and that's our secret place. But when it comes into view we both stop and look at it. Like we've never seen it before.

The waterfall is large by island standards. And it never seems to stop falling. Ever. Like magic, it's always there for us when we come. Of course, it has to stop sometimes. It's made of rainwater in a pool at the top of the highest peak.

But reality hides that little fact from us. So we refuse to believe it. It's not really water, just like we're not really people. It's magic.

"We haven't been in here in a long time," Rory says, echoing my earlier thought.

"No," I say. "We got busy, I guess. Forgot that magic lives here. But I want us to remember today."

She slips her tank top over her head, her eyes burning with the same desire I remember from our first summer together after I told her everything. She unclasps her bra, and that falls down onto the path with her shirt.

I don't need to stare at her breasts anymore. I see them all the time. They're a part of me now. So I stare at her eyes. Because I can't ever know enough about what's behind those eyes. There is no memory that can replace the real thing when I look into her eyes.

"Five," she says, lifting up my shirt.

I raise my arms and let her pull it over my head.

She doesn't look at my chest. She looks right into my eyes. Just like I did her.

"What?" I ask, wanting her to speak so bad. I always want to hear her voice. Even though I hear it every day. Have heard it every way.

Her eyes dart back and forth to each of mine. Like she's searching for something but she can't find it.

"What?" I ask again.

But she shakes her head. Smiles. "I love you."

We jump into the pool of rainwater that never ends and go under. The water is clear. Not as clear as the ocean down below, but perfectly clear. Like everything else in this place. She takes my hand while we're still under and then kicks her feet to swim.

I follow, clinging to her fingertips like I'll never let go. Like I can't ever get close enough and she might slip away.

We come up once. Just long enough to grab a breath of air and smile at each other. And then, like we've done this millions of times throughout eternity, we duck back under the water, letting the force of the waterfall pound our backs, and resurface inside the secret we've been hiding since we first found the magic here at the top of our personal paradise.

She lets got of my hand and I have to sigh. Because I hate letting go. Even here, where no one and nothing can touch us. She places both hands on the flat, smooth slab of rock that reminds me so much of our rock along the spring behind Sparrow's house it almost hurts, and lifts herself out of the water. Dripping. Her nipples peaking up from the coolness of the cave.

I follow, and we stand there. The humidity enveloping us like a blanket. Making our skin prickle until a chill runs up our bodies and we shiver together.

"God," I say, taking her face in my hands again. "You're so beautiful."

She lets out a long breath of air and says, "Fuck me."

"Gladly," I say, pulling on the button of her shorts. She wiggles her hips until I can pull them over. They are wet and stick to her skin. But every moment is delicious.

I feel her thighs. The taut muscles in her legs. And then brush my fingertips along the back of her knees.

"Fuck me," she says again. "Fuck me. Fuck me. Fuck me."

She begins tugging on my shorts now too. The button. The zipper. She tugs them down my legs. Hard, impatient. Desperate.

After all these years, she is still desperate for me.

I lift her up and she wraps her arms and legs around me. Hugs me with every part of herself.

And when I sit down on the flat, smooth rock, I'm already inside her. Her hips are already rocking. Her fingertips running across my scalp, tousling my hair. My fingertips pinching her nipples, making her gasp.

And I do exactly what she told me to do. I fuck her.
But it's not fucking. It's love.

# CHAPTER TWENTY

# MAC

Ellie is blindfolded.

I had to convince her to come away with me. She was hell-bent on staying up at the house to wait for Five's twins to finish testing. But... well, I'm known for my creative ways into getting women to do what I want.

Plus, she likes the blindfold game. We do it all the time.

She stumbles a little as I lead her down the path to the marina. "I got you," I say. And I do. She doesn't fall.

"Where are we going?"

"Date day, remember?"

"Oh, God." But she laughs. So I know she likes my little surprise.

When we get to the dock I help her up into Corporate's boat, which is called *Hidden Treasure*—dumbass—and it's not even a boat. Fucking small yacht is what it is.

I pull Ellie's blindfold down so she can see where we are.

"We're going somewhere?"

"Not somewhere, Mrs. Perfect. We're gonna have an adventure. West told me about some caves on an island nearby and we're gonna go explore them."

She leans up on her tiptoes to kiss my lips. "You're gonna spelunk me?"

"Yeah." I laugh with her. "I'm gonna spelunk the shit out of you. So just put on that bikini for the ride over…" I waggle my eyebrows at her. "Or not." More waggling "And relax. I got this, Eloise."

"Eloise." She snorts. "You hardly ever call me that and this is the second time in two days. What's up with you, Mr. Perfect?"

"I like to surprise you. And I don't do it enough, so today should be a day of surprises."

She slips her hands underneath my shirt and gazes up into my eyes. "Maybe I don't like surprises."

"You do. Which is why our date day is gonna be nothing but new things. A constant stream of new things. A cornucopia of fun and whole lot of sexy times."

"Perfect," she coos.

"That's Mr. Perfect to you."

She laughs and playfully pushes me away. "I'm gonna change. Make sure you ditch that shirt before I get back."

Yeah, I decide, watching her ass wiggle as she hops down the steps to the lounge area. I'm gonna remember this day, I think. An entire day alone with Ellie in paradise? Doing shit we never do? Perfect indeed.

I press start on Corporate's nav system and then walk into the galley to see what he's got as far as drinks go. I spy a wine cooler under the counter and choose a bottle of champagne—why not do it up right, right?—and then grab two glasses from the cupboard, and some grapes from the fridge.

"Mr. Perfect," Ellie says behind me. "Why are you still dressed?"

I turn around, opening my mouth to beg forgiveness, and then just let it hang there.

She's not in a bikini. She's naked.

"You look delicious."

"What are you doing?" she asks, eyeing the counter where all my delights are lined up. "I hope you've got butter in there."

I laugh. Like pretty loud. Then whip my shirt off and walk over to her, my hands on her hips, but just briefly, because they want to wander over the curve of her ass. "That was the best day ever. You know that?"

"I dunno," she whispers into my neck as I pull her close. "We've had some pretty good ones since then."

"Yeah, but you gotta admit, butter was a sick idea."

"Sick?" she says, feigning ignorance. "As in cool as fuck? Or as in you're one twisted dude?"

"Both," I say, chuckling.

"You blew my mind that day. In fact, you blow my mind every day, Mac. From the day I met you, I've been having fun."

"All the days?" I ask, hitching up one eyebrow.

"Well, I missed you those couple of months we were apart while I was writing my book. But they were necessary. So I could figure things out."

"Like what?" I ask. "What did you figure out, Ellie?"

"That you really are perfect. In every way. And I know I've been moody lately, and I'm sorry. I should appreciate you and all the good things in my life more. But it's just a little overwhelming. I didn't expect this, ya know? Look at Ivy."

"What about her?"

"Well, she and Nolan didn't even plan for a baby and yet they have a simply adorable little girl now. I feel... jealous. And then I feel guilty for feeling jealous because Ivy is one of my best friends. So... I don't like it. Not at all. And I don't like the feeling that something I really want might be a monumental struggle to achieve. And hard work and determination won't be enough to overcome it. I want a baby, Mac. So bad, it hurts. I can't explain it. And it probably doesn't make sense to you—"

"It does," I say, brushing some hair away from her eyes. "But the universe knows what it's doing, Ellie. Sometimes it likes to throw curve balls. Make life a struggle. So you can come out the other end and appreciate it more than you did before. We just gotta trust that things will turn out the way they're supposed to."

She rests her head on my chest and I hug her tight. "I love you," she says. "And I can't wait to be your Mrs. tomorrow."

We just stand like that. Holding each other close and enjoying the moment. And then I pull away and lift her up. She wraps her arms and legs around me as I walk us outside into the sunshine, and I place her down on the deck of the boat and just... look at her.

She scissors her legs back and forth, blushing up at me. And then she opens them wide, and says, "Down here, Perfect. I need you right now, right here," as she taps her pussy with her fingertips.

Jesus. My wife-to-be is fuck hot.

"Come on," she urges. "Don't be shy."

I laugh as I drop to my knees and crawl towards her. Then I reach for her knees, shoot her a devilish grin, and place both hands, palms down, on her thighs as I descend into her sweetness.

Her back arches as I suck on her, flicking my tongue back and forth across her clit.

"Mac," she moans.

"Ellie," I whisper, making her arch her back again. She fists my hair and I look up from between her legs and watch her as I lick and suck her into ecstasy. I want to touch her everywhere at once. I want my cock deep inside her. I want to fuck her hard and soft at the same time. I just want... her. Forever.

I pull back and she whines, "Noooo." But then I'm kissing my way up her body. My lips fluttering against the smooth, tanned skin of her stomach. Both hands squeezing her breasts as I crawl up, and press my hard dick into her.

"Take these off," she says, tugging on my swim trunks.

But fuck that. As soon as they're down far enough to release my cock, I push into her. Sweep my arms under her back and hold her close to me as I go deeper.

She moans, her hands wrapping around my back, her fingernails digging into my shoulders, leaving marks that I can't wait to look at tomorrow. So I can remember this perfect day with my perfect wife.

I prop myself up on my elbows so I can gaze down at her beautiful face and then I go slow. I push into her, deep. And pull out, almost all the way out. Until she grabs on to me just to make sure that doesn't happen. Her legs wrap around my waist, holding me there, so I can't pull out.

I look at her and we laugh together. God, I want to do everything with her. Every. Thing.

I lean down and kiss her nose. Then each of her cheeks. I kiss one eye. Then the other. Her forehead. I start fucking her again. Just slow this time. In and out. Agonizingly slow, until she's lifting up her hips in a demand for more and thrusting against me.

"You're gonna make me happy forever," she says, her voice low and throaty with desire.

"Yes," I promise her. "Yes."

"And whatever happens, happens."

"That's right, babe. We're gonna let fate take us and no matter how much it throws at us, we're gonna come out the other side holding hands."

She closes her eyes, bites her lip, and then we come together.

We must've fallen asleep after that because we wake to a boat horn blaring at us.

I lift my head, shield my eyes from the sun, and catch people yelling and screaming as they go by.

They're smiling and laughing and pointing. And that's when I realize we're still naked.

I wave and slump back down, pulling Ellie to my chest.

"You exhibitionist." She laughs.

"Hey, I still have pants on."

She slaps me on the shoulder and then turns around so she's on her stomach. "Is that the island?"

It's only then that I realize the boat has stopped and we're just bobbing up and down in front of our destination. "Must be it," I say. "Should we stay here all day? Fuck a little more, drink champagne, and eat grapes? Or should we go on an adventure?"

"I vote adventure."

"Me too," I say.

The perfect day *must* end in an adventure.

"Let's see..." I say, looking through all Corporate's storage drawers. "There's got to be flashlights somewhere."

"Are you sure this is safe?" Ellie asks.

"Sure," I say. I really have no idea. But I'm not gonna tell her that. "West said he took Ethan and Tori on the way here. And Ethan loved it so much, they're gonna do it again on the way home. If Ethan can spelunk, we can too." I shoot her a smile of confidence.

"I dunno. Ethan is like Tarzan. That kid can do anything athletic."

I think about that for a second. He is kinda wild. Then I picture Tori spelunking. "Tori did it too. And she's what I'd call high-maintenance. You know, 'OMG, I might break a nail,' kinda girl."

Ellie scrunches up her face at me. "I don't think you really know her."

I wave that off. I actually can picture Tori spelunking, if only to prove to Weston that she can do it better than he can. "We'll be fine."

"Hey, there's some people coming out. I'm gonna go ask them what it's like."

"Sure," I say. "Meet you down there."

I find the flashlights, which are actually headlights—leave it to fucking Corporate to be prepared for an adventure—and then I hop onto the dock and walk towards Ellie, where she's taking to a couple in a boat. They take off before I get there and Ellie is smiling again, so I figure they told her it was safe. "So?" I say.

"They say the entrance is just right over there. Then there's a red rope you follow into the cave so you don't get lost, and some steps and ladders and shit. And when you get to the top, you can see like… the entire world. Sounds totally cool. I'm in."

"Perfect," I say, not even minding the pun. I take her hand and lead her away. "Let's go. With any luck we'll get to the top, climb back down, and be back on the boat fucking and drinking to watch the sunset."

We walk through some tall grass towards a large, dark hole in the hillside. "I guess that's it," I say.

"Looks like it."

We're just passing through the entrance, looking for the guide rope, when a shooting pain has me slapping at my neck. "Jesus fuck!" I say. "What the hell was that?"

"What happened?" Ellie asks, panicked. "What's wrong?"

"I think something just stung me!"

We both hear the buzzing at the same time and look up to see a swarm of bees, or wasps, or fucking horse flies, for all I know. "Run!" I say, pulling her inside the cave with me. We haul ass until it really gets too dark to see, and then we stop, panting and out of breath.

"Holy shit," Ellie says. "Those people could've warned us about the damn bees!"

"I think they were like mutant bees, Ells. I have a huge lump on my neck."

"Let me see," she says, putting on her headlight and shining it on my wound. "Ohhhhh," is her only response.

"What?" I ask. "What's it look like."

Ellie just stares at it, her eyes wide.

"Ellie!" I say. "Is it bad?"

She nods her head and then says, "No."

I laugh. Even though the fucking sting hurts like hell, and I have to press my fingers into my skin to dull the pain. "Which is it, Nurse Perfect?"

She cocks her head at me and her left eye does this little twitch, which is her tell that she's about to lie. "It's just... a little red, that's all. And swollen. And... is that pus? Jesus. How could a bee sting get this bad so quick? Should we go back?"

"Back? For a fucking bee sting? Nah," I say, shaking it off. "It's fine. I'm not allergic. It'll be fine by the time we're done."

"Are you sure?" Ellie says, giving my sting the stink-eye.

"I'm sure," I say, pointing to the red guide rope. "Look, there's the rope. Let's go spelunk the fuck out of this cave."

"OK," Ellie says. "If you're sure."

"I'm sure. I got this, babe."

We walk a little farther in and then notice the ground is squishy. "Is the whole thing wet?" Ellie asks. "Like, should we have on boots or something?"

I laugh it off. "Boots. We're fine. Just a little sea water. This cave must have an outlet to the ocean, that's all."

"OK," Ellie says as we go a little further, until the water is up to our ankles. "But I think I see... *things* in that water."

I follow her headlight beam down to my shoes and see—"Holy fuck!" I grab her and run, pulling her along behind me. "Get on the rocks! Quick! Before those snakes get us!"

I lift her up, then scramble up behind her, panting. "What the hell? Those people couldn't mention this fucking cave is filled with snakes? What is this? Some kind of wild Indiana Jones adventure?"

"Calm down, Mr. Fraidy-Cat. I think they're just eels."

"Just eels?" I say. "Eels?"

"The tide is coming in," Ellie says. "Look."

I'm afraid to look. Every time I look at what she's pointing at, something stupid happens. But I do anyway. Because that's the kind of man I am. And sure as shit, there's waves crashing against the rocks. "Where the fuck is all this water coming from?"

"Like you said, there's some kind of ocean outlet, I bet."

"Well, that fucking tide had better be low when it's time to leave. I'm not swimming through eels."

Elle chuckles. "Come on, there's the rope. We're in the right place, at least. We just go up these rock steps and then there'll be a ladder to get to the top, right?"

"Yeah," I say. "Sure." But nothing those people told us has been even remotely accurate so far. So I'm not hopeful.

"Is this the steps?" Elli asks. I shine my head light and see some giant stacked stones.

"You think?" I ask her.

"I dunno. They just look like rocks to me. But that's the way the rope goes. So we better follow it."

So we do. We climb up the steps, which are closely spaced for a while, but eventually they stop being stacked stones and turn into boulders, each one taller than the next, until I have to make a step with my hand and hoist Ellie up to the next one.

When I follow her up, I'm out of breath and I'm getting a very bad feeling about this cave trip. "Maybe we're not cut out for spelunking?" I ask, laughing.

"Maybe not, Mr. We're Going On An Adventure Today. But we're probably halfway up, don't you think? And I bet the tide hasn't even gone down yet, so we might as well go all the way."

140

The next few boulders have rope ladders to get up them. Ellie shoots me a dubious look. Because ya know what? Rope ladders aren't all that easy to use.

"I'll be right behind you, OK?"

I get another hesitant look from her.

"Looking at your ass, wishing we were back on the boat, fucking and getting drunk."

She looks up. There's like a teeny tiny light up there. "Is that the top, ya think?"

"Yup," I say with as much confidence as I can muster. And the whole time we're doing this I'm picturing eight-year-old Ethan. Tarzan is right. How the fuck did that kid do this? Even with Tori and West's help? "Come on, I think there's like an opening up there so we can rest for a minute before we do the final ascent."

The remaining steps—which makes me want to punch those people on the dock at this point, because these things are giant boulders, not steps—are like eight feet tall and one of them has no rope ladder at all. Ellie shines her headlight around until she finds remnants of rope and sighs.

"We're not gonna make it, Mac. We'll have to climb down after all, I guess."

"Fuck that," I say. "I didn't get stung by a killer hornet, wade through a pit of snakes, and then climb up Mount fucking Everest for nothing. We're gonna get to the top and see the goddamned world if it's the last thing I do. Get on my back," I say, crouching down. "Then grab that stump right there and hold on while I stand up. Then you can stand on my shoulders and I'll push you the rest of the way up."

"How will you get up?"

I sigh, and look back at the rope remnants. "I'll throw that up to you, you tie it off on something, and then I'll climb up that way."

"Jesus. Is it really worth all this? I mean, how great can that view be?"

"It's motherfucking spectacular. And we're gonna enjoy it before we descend back into the evil pit of darkness."

She laughs. "You've never even seen it."

"It doesn't matter. We're gonna spelunk the shit out of this cave. If Ethan can do it, we can do it. We're adults, for fuck's sake. He's like... a midget. Now get on my back."

She does. And she balances on my shoulders when I stand up. But she kicks my sting—bite—whatever the fuck it is, and I feel something ooze out of it. I don't even want to think about that, so I just grab her ass and push her the rest of the way.

She scrambles over the edge, then I throw the rope up and after what seems like for-fucking-ever, she says, "OK. It's secure."

I'd like to say I'm a great rope climber. But fuck it. I'm not. But I make it and then we're in the opening and the top is right above us.

"I hate to tell you this," Ellie says, laughing.

"What now?"

"That's not a ladder."

I look at where her headlight is pointing and nope. Sure fuckin' isn't. It's just a rope with knots in it. Like the kind of thing you see hanging off a tree limb that's used to swing over a body of water.

"Shit," I say.

"And I think we're been in here a long time," Ellie says. "Because I think the light from the outside is fading."

I check my watch. "Five. Hours. You have got to be kidding me."

Ellie just laughs.

And hell, what else can you do? I laugh too.

That last climb is torture. But she's doing OK in front of me. And I actually do have a great view of her ass. So I just go with it. We're about six feet from the opening when I smell something rancid.

"What the hell is that smell?" Ellie asks.

"I dunno, but it's rank, right?"

"Horrible."

And that's when the bats attack.

At this point, we're just like, fuck it. We laugh the rest of the way up, swatting the bats away as they flutter around us. Ellie screams, "They're gonna get in my hair!" because that's what everyone says when bats show up, and then we laugh harder.

We pull ourselves up out of that cave and I vow, as we collapse into the tall grass at the top of the island, that never will I ever spelunk again.

That's when we see the kid staring down at us like we're crazy freaks as he opens his mouth and a sucker falls out. "Mommy! It's a cave monster!" And then he runs away screaming.

"What the hell?" Ellie says. "How the hell did that kid get up here?"

We stand up, walk over a ridge, smelling like we just came out of a... well, bat cave. And see about two dozen people milling about taking pictures of the low-hanging sun.

"Look," Ellie says, pointing at a sign.

"Cave Trail," I say, reading the sign. And it's paved. It's a goddamned sidewalk. And when we go over to it and look down, we see a nice, easy path filled with tourists making their way up to the top of the island.

We just laugh. And laugh. And laugh. I take her hand and lead her over to the edge of the cliff, and we sink into the grass, and watch the sun as it sits on the top of the water, blanketing it with a cone of orange, and red, and yellow.

Ellie sighs and says, "Some things are worth the struggle, ya know?"

And I say, "Yeah," as I give her hand a squeeze. "Some things are."

# CHAPTER TWENTY-ONE

# NOLAN

So this is how it went.

I said OK. Because it's a tiny fucking pig, right? And even though there's a ton of big pigs the girls were right. The big pigs aren't interested in the little pig. The little pig is definitely gonna die. So I'm all busting into gonna-save-the-pig mode and shit, walking out on the beach, taking cover behind palm trees when I can, sneaking up on the thing...

And just as I'm about to grab it, the big daddy pig sees me.

And in that same moment, both girls start screaming, "Run!"

I'm like... shit. Fucking pigs can run fast. I never knew that. And halfway into that thought I'm turning, and my feet are doing their thing, and then all pig hell breaks loose! There's no longer one big daddy pig, but like, eleven of them. All chasing me down the beach, and then I see Five's girls climbing up these palm trees like a couple of goddamned monkeys—you know how they shimmy up a palm tree? Anyway, they got up into trees. Like they've done this a million times and no big deal.

But me? I don't know how to shimmy up a fucking palm tree, so I gotta keep running for the next tree, which is normal and actually has branches.

And that big daddy pig took my shoe on my way up. Took my motherfucking shoe!

145

So now I'm down a shoe, I'm stuck in a tree, and a dozen giant pigs are rooting around at the bottom like they're just gonna wait me out.

I think I've heard that pigs eat people. "Hey!" I call to the girls. "Do pigs eat people?"

They just laugh at me. From the safety of their palm trees. Where there are no pigs waiting them out.

So I yell, "Hey! How long will they stay?"

And then Mathilda and Louise exchange little sneaky grins. You've seen it before, when one person looks at another person and they have some kind of secret conversation in their minds. And then Louise nods, and Mathilda nods, and then they both start knocking coconuts off the trees, which scares the pigs and makes them go investigate. And then Mathilda yells, "Run!"

And I'm like... fuck that. I'm staying right here in my goddamned tree.

Not to mention I can't leave them here. Fucking Five will shoot my ass if I get his girls killed by rabid pigs.

So I yell, "No." Which does nothing for the situation at all.

Mathilda yells, "You run and then throw rocks at them from the other direction. We'll escape when they go investigate."

I hesitate.

Louise says, "We do this every day, Romantic. Man up and do your job."

Really? She's like five years old. They let them run wild with insane pigs all day?

"Go!" Mathilda yells again. Louise is still knocking coconuts off her tree, so the whole gang of pigs is busy, so I mutter, "Fuck it," and jump down, kicking off my other shoe, because what the fuck good is one shoe

146

anyway? And then I look around for some rocks, and start throwing them the other direction. And sure enough, the herd of pigs takes off to go check shit out.

Then like that, in a snap, Louise and Mathilda are scrambling back down their respective palm trees and they burst into the jungle where I'm waiting, laughing like… well, fucking kids.

"That was not cool," I say in my brand-new stern dad voice. I'm not very good at that voice because Bronte is only six months old, so I haven't had a chance to really use it yet. So they just keep laughing. "Come on, we're going back to your house and I'm telling your father on you."

They snicker even harder now.

"What?" I ask, turning around.

"You have to get us that pig."

"Yeah," Louise says. "You didn't get our pig yet."

"Your dad is gonna kill me if I get you killed by pigs."

"Pfffft," Mathilda says. "Our dad is never gonna know."

"Yeah," Louise adds. "Because you're never gonna tell him." Somehow she's got that pointy stick in her hand again, and she thrusts it towards me like she's gonna take me out with it.

"And we did tell you to run," Mathilda says. Like this makes everything OK.

"While they were charging me!" I say. "As if I couldn't figure that out. And don't point that stick at me!"

"We're just gonna have to go to plan B, OK?" Mathilda says, like this is obvious.

I sneer at them. Little miscreants. "What's plan B?"

"We lure them away with food and then take the baby pig when they're busy eating."

"Why didn't we do that first?" I ask. "So much better than run out there and grab him."

"Because we wanted to watch you run," Louise says.

"That's not why," Mathilda says, shooting her sister a look that says, *Shut up*, because she knows I'm about to bail out on the whole stupid plan. "It's because we have to smear mud all over our bodies so they can't smell us when we leave the food. And we didn't think you'd want to take a mud bath. So plan A had to come first."

I think about this. I'm not very excited about smearing mud all over my body, that's for sure. So yeah, I probably would've said no before I realized these pigs are more like an LA street gang than some harmless tropical oddities this part of the Bahamas is famous for.

"Come on, Nolan," Louise says, doing that pouty thing.

"Yeah," Mathilda says. "We're gonna help you. We promise."

I look up at the sun. It's gotta be noon already. "I just want to spend some time with my wife. And learn how to be a better dad to a girl, that's all."

"I know exactly how you can do that," Mathilda says.

"How?"

"You gotta get us that pig first," Louise adds. "Then... we help you."

I sigh. Because I just really want to make this day special for Ivy and I've got no ideas on how to do that. So fuck it. "What do we feed the pigs?"

They both clap their hands and jump up and down. "Fruit!" Louise says.

"Yeah, we just go pick bananas and mangos and put them in a pile. They'll come running. They always do."

"But first we roll in the mud," Louise says, but she's got a little glint in her eye that makes me suspicious. "And *then* we feed them the fruit and steal the baby pig. Just like that."

"They won't let the little pig eat," Mathilda says. "So they'll leave it alone and you can go in and get it."

"We'll watch your back," Louise chirps. "And we'll have rocks to throw to distract them this time if they go after you."

"Fine." I sigh. "But I'm spending one hour on this and that's it. One. Then I'm gone. I can't waste this day. I just want to spend some time with my wife."

"Deal," they both say, spitting on their hands and holding them out for me to shake.

Jesus. I spit on mine and shake them. Five's girls are not the little princesses I imagined them to be.

Then we go trekking through the jungle looking for fruit.

I try not to look at the sun, knowing that more than an hour has already passed by the time we collect enough fruit to feed a gang of pigs, but I can't help it. My perfect day is wasting away.

"OK," Mathilda says, leading me up to the mud puddle. "This is where the pigs roll. So all we gotta do is roll in the mud until we're covered, then sit in the sun for a minute to let it dry, and then we'll go get that baby pig."

I give up. There's just no fighting these girls. They want that stupid pig and they're not letting me off the hook until we get it.

Louise goes first. She's all too eager to get into that goop. And a minute later she's covered and smells like, well pig shit, if I'm being honest. Mathilda goes next, and then it's my turn.

"What the fuck am I doing?" I mumble, dropping to my knees and lying back in the thick, disgusting, slop.

"You're making sure you have the perfect date for your wife, Romantic," Mathilda says.

I glare at her, and then Louise splashes me with mud until I'm covered, and I'm sure, like one hundred percent positive, that my date is never happening. I'm a total failure at this date day thing. And I bet all the other guys are having the best time ever. And it was my idea! Fuckers.

"OK," Louise says, standing back to look at me. She smiles, blasting me with that adorable gap that used to be her front teeth. "You're ready."

"Let's do this," Mathilda says, picking up her pointy stick.

I follow them back to the beach, hoping—praying—that the pigs will be gone. On a whole other island, maybe. Or swimming in the ocean, so we can just stop this stupid plan before it goes off the rails.

But no such luck. They are all snorting around on the shore looking for crabs or something.

"There he is!" Louise squeals.

Mathilda hushes her with a well-placed hand over her mouth and says, "OK, Romantic, you go down that way and wait. We'll lure them away with the food and then run. And while we're doing that, you grab that pig and meet us back here. Got it?"

It sounds so simple. I mean, I know it's crazy, but she makes it sound so simple. So I just go, "OK," and stalk my way down where she was just pointing.

They take off in the jungle, leaving me alone. And part of me wonders how the hell I let two small girls talk me into such a crazy plan in the first place.

But I'm here now. Covered in stinking pig shit—I'm pretty sure that wasn't mud—and that little pig is only about twenty yards away.

That's when I hear Louise calling out from the other end of the beach. "Here, piggy-piggy-piggy! Here, piggy-piggy-piggy!"

She's nuts.

Then Mathilda throws bananas and mangos at the bigger pigs, who turn, snorting and huffing, toward their attacker. I wince, expecting a full-fledged charge to happen next, but then... they just walk calmly over to the bouncing fruit and start eating. The whole gang of them.

The little pig tries to get in there, but one bigger pig gives it a kick and it goes reeling backwards with a squeal.

Fuckers. They're hurting my baby pig!

I glance down the beach, where Mathilda is waving at me to go grab it, and come out of the jungle looking like the Swamp Thing incarnate.

I'm stalking up behind them, carefully... slowly... and as I'm holding my hand out for that little pig, it occurs to me I really should've brought some fruit with me so I could feed it.

And that's when Louise yells, "Run!"

Shit! There are at least six boars coming at me. I sprint to the piglet, scoop it up like a football, tuck it under my arm, and take off for our meeting place like I'm about to make the winning touchdown.

"Look out!" Mathilda says.

And when I glance over to my left I see that huge daddy pig coming straight at me. I swerve, barely missing his teeth as he gnashes the air, and then get hit with a rock. "Ow!" I yell. "Motherfucker! Watch where you're throwing those things!"

"Sorry!" Louise calls from down the beach, just as another rocks pelts me in the ear.

But that daddy pig isn't giving up so easy. He's right behind me now, and then I see Mathilda up in front, hiding in the jungle with her arms out, like she wants me to toss the pig to her so she can take it over the goal line.

And I don't know what I'm thinking, but I do it. I fucking throw the pig and it goes sailing through the air, squealing and twisting, and then she catches him!

That's when I trip and fall. And get trampled by daddy pig as he takes off into the jungle after Mathilda.

I shake it off and get up running, because I know that injury won't hit me until later anyway, and there's no way I'm walking back into Five's place with the news of his daughter's demise from pig. So I take off after them, scooping up rocks as I run, and find daddy pig snorting and howling as he stalks up to Mathilda and her piglet.

"Yaaaaaahhhhh," comes from off to my right, and that would be crazy-ass Louise, spear in hand, as she charges the pig at full speed. She throws her spear, which hits the boar in his side, but of course, it's a fucking stick and not a spear. So it bounces right off his thick hide.

Jesus Christ. We're all gonna die if I don't get this shit handled quick.

So I handle it.

I grab another rock, wind my arm up like I'm about to throw the last strike in game seven of the World Series, and hurl it as hard as I can, right at that pig's head.

It bounces off too. And for a second I think that fucker's made of steel or something.

But then the boar wobbles, his eyes crossing, and just... falls over.

"Is he dead?" I ask, panting out the words.

"No," Mathilda says, running at me. "Come on! We gotta go! He'll be up in a few seconds!"

So the three of us run and we run hard. We run like kids. Like this is a game we're playing and we just won.

And we laugh. Even the little pig laughs. We laugh like this is the best day of our collective lives.

Because it might be. It just might be.

I don't even argue when Mathilda tells me to stand still while she hoses me off. Of course I need to be hosed off. I rolled around in pig muck. And my consolation prize is that I get to hose them off afterward. And the pig, who goes squealing away into the bushes, setting off a wild pig hunt that is almost—not quite, but almost—as exciting as the first one.

When we're done with that, and we're lying on the grass in front of their princess palace, I sigh and realize the day is gone. "My big plans for today are bust, I think."

"No," Louise says, propping herself up on her elbow. "We're just getting started, Nolan. You gotta go home, shower, change, and then bring your wife and baby back here. Leave it to us. We'll take care of everything."

I shoot her the stink-eye. "The whole point of date day was to have time *alone*."

"Leave it to *us*," Mathilda says. "Seriously."

"You know," Louise says, "everything would go a lot faster if you just gave in and did what you were told."

And then they snicker like that's a fantastic joke.

"Would it?" I say, wondering.

"My mommy tells my daddy that all the time," Louise says.

"She always wins," Mathilda says. "So she's right. Daddy should just give in first. Then they could skip the arguments."

153

Fuck it. I'm exhausted. I don't even have it in me to fight with them anymore. So I drag myself up, walk back to our bungalow, and go inside.

"What the—" And that's as far as Ivy gets because she breaks into a laugh.

"I've had quite a day," I say.

"What happened to your shoes?"

"You wouldn't believe me if I told you."

"Is that mud in your hair?" She's still laughing.

"Yes, Mrs. Romantic. Not only is that mud, but a very special kind of mud. Found only in the wallow holes of island pigs."

"Pigs?"

Now Bronte is laughing at me too.

"Pigs," I say. And then I stop talking. Stop thinking. And just look at them. Bronte's cheeks are pink, like she's been outside today. And Ivy's skin is glowing with the radiance you only see after a day in the sun. They are so fucking beautiful. I want to hug her. Hold her. Kiss her. Both of them. But I smell. So I just say, "What'd you guys do today?"

"Hung out at the pool with Five's girls. They're delightful. What did you do?" She's eyeing my still-wet clothes like it's a puzzle that needs to be solved.

"I too spent the day with Five's girls. The younger hoodlums, not the twins, obviously." And then I smile. "It was the best day."

She sets Bronte down on the floor so she can play with some toys, and comes towards me.

"Stay back," I warn her. "I smell like... a nasty, disgusting, daddy pig."

She wraps her arms around me anyway, kisses me on the lips, and then says, "I love you. And even though tomorrow is what we're calling the real wedding, our real wedding happened last year. While I was pregnant. And only you and I were there. And it was perfect, Mr. Romantic. Just perfect. So I'm going along with this wedding to make you and my father see eye to eye on this transfer of power, but I'd just like to go on record that I don't need it. None of it."

I smile and kiss her. "I know, Ivy. And I had planned to spend the whole day with you and just you, but I got wrangled into the most fun ever. With two very non-traditional little girls whose ideas of what it means to be a little girl just upended my world. So even though we didn't have the day, we're gonna have our night no matter what. We're gonna have to take Bronte along with us, and the place I'm taking you isn't anyone's idea of a good time"— she laughs—"but we're going anyway. So let me take a shower and then we can go."

An hour later the three of us walk back to the Princess Palace. Bronte is half asleep in my arms and Ivy is telling me all about how she wants Bronte's hair braided for the wedding tomorrow, and how her little dress has to be done up just right, and all kinds of wedding shit that I have no clue about, but love to listen to, when we come up to the front door of the oversized playhouse.

"Here?" Ivy laughs.

"I told you it wasn't anyone's idea of a good time." But in my head I take that back. Five's kids have probably had millions of days like this growing up. This little house is the definition of a good time if you're one of them. "Just trust me," I say, even though I have no clue what I'm gonna find inside.

"Welcome to the Princess Palace," Mathilda says, opening the door.

"Ohhhhh," Ivy says, looking at me. "Fancy!"

I grin, because not only is Mathilda dressed up like a proper little princess, complete with silver fairy wings and a sparkling crown, she's got on a long white summer dress that just… just says everything about what it means to be a little girl, and then again, nothing at all about what it means to be a little girl. Her skin is tanned and glowing, just like Ivy's. And her hair has been washed, brushed and swept back with a white cotton headband.

Louise appears then, looking like the most perfect little lady in pink version of what Mathilda is wearing. And I can't stop my glance over at Bronte to imagine what she'll be like when she's that age.

I cannot fucking wait.

"Come in!" Louise says. "We've got your table ready."

Ivy and I exchange smiles, and even Bronte is awake and looking around at the magical place her parents have brought her.

It is magical. All the toys have been put away. The small table has been newly set for tea with their tiny china set. There's classical music playing from a tape recorder. And in the corner, sitting atop a pink velvet cushion, is the piglet. I almost die when it snorts at me.

"A tea party?" Ivy says, catching on to the theme.

"Yeah," I say, smiling so fucking big. "A romantic date for my girls."

I decide Corporate was right.

I already know how to throw a football, but every father of a princess needs to learn how to throw a tea party.

And I had the best teachers ever.

CHAPTER TWENTY-TWO

# WEST

I surface from the water and my memory of that first day with the Conrads and see Tori and Ethan still on the rock.

"Dad!" Ethan laughs. "I already got one!" He holds up a fish. I can't make out what it is from here and I'm not all that familiar with the tropical fish anyway, so I don't even try. I just wave from the water and continue to swim.

The ocean feels like coming home every time. And maybe that life wasn't so bad. I mean, being that kid, on that Nantucket beach, diving every day to feed myself... it made me into the man I am now.

But no adult wants that for a kid, theirs or not. And I don't want that for Ethan. I want to give him all the things the Conrads gave me without all the bad things that came with it.

"Hey, kid," I say, dragging myself up on to the rock. "Good job." I ruffle his wet hair and then look at Tori. She's smiling. She loves him. So much. And even though she's pregnant with our first biological child, there's no way Ethan will ever come in second. And I know that's impossible to say, since when you have two, they can't both always be first. But she will make it happen. And Ethan will grow up loved, and valued, and respected for who he is and not what we might want to turn him into.

Which then makes me feel guilty. Because I wish—very much—that he'd stop all this stuff he's doing and just settle down.

But what if that never happens? What if this is just who he is? What if he never stops sneaking out at night? Or feeling like he has to provide for people? Or—

"What are you thinking about, Weston Conrad?"

I sigh and pull her into me. She's warm and dry, and I'm cold and wet. But she lets me do it anyway. "Just... stuff. Ya know?"

"Stuff like me?" Ethan says. Offhandedly. Not even bothering to look over his shoulder at us. He's always like that. Just kinda... honest and open. Not many people have those two qualities as their default setting, so it's a little disarming when you encounter it.

I'm fully disarmed at the moment, but I figure the only way to handle honesty is with honesty. So I say, "There's gonna be a whole party of people here tonight. Are you planning on feeding all of them?"

He laughs. Says, "Yup. As soon as you show me how to get these lobsters. They're prickly, look!" He holds out his hand and shows me his palm, which has little spots of blood from where he's been trying to catch lobster and got stuck with their spines. "But I got him." And he points to the cooler of seawater with one lobster already inside it.

"Well, I'll show you how to do it the right way, how's that?"

"Yes!" he says, doing a fist-pump. "I'm gonna be as good as you one day."

"Better," I say, looking at Tori.

She says, "You know, I think I'll leave you two here to fish for a while. I see a white sandy beach calling my name."

She gives me a kiss, tucks her sunglasses into her shorts, and then dives off the rock and starts swimming for the beach.

That's my cue to get to the bottom of what's going on with Ethan, so I clear my throat and say, "So…" And that's as far as I get.

"So Mom wants you to talk to me about sneaking out at night and doing stuff kids shouldn't do, right?"

"Uh… yeah."

"Well, Dad, look." He redirects his attention from his fishing over to me, lifts up his mirrored aviator sunglasses—where the fuck did he get those?—and says, "I'm just being me. And I know it's not normal. They've all told me that over the years." And then he lowers the glasses again, hiding his eyes.

I laugh. Because he's eight. How many years can people have been telling him this?

"But I can't help who I am."

"Who are you?" I ask.

"Ethan," he says. "Ethan Conrad."

"Before that, Ethan. Who were you before that?"

"Ethan Wright."

I know his real last name. But that's not what I meant. So I sigh, frustrated and unsure how to have this conversation.

He looks back to his fishing. "Ethan Wright was a lonely kid."

"Why?" I ask, relieved that he gets me. He knows what I'm after and he's taking the initiative. Even though he shouldn't have to because he's… *eight.*

159

"He had a brother," Ethan says.

"He did? I mean, you did?" This third-person thing is freaking me out a little.

"Yeah." Ethan looks at me, but all I see is myself. Both in who he is and in the mirrors covering his eyes. "He was twelve."

"Was twelve? So he's..."

"Dead now," Ethan says. "But I saw it coming."

"You did?" I ask, my heart breaking and beating fast at the same time.

"Yeah," Ethan says. "He had cancer."

"Jesus. Where are your parents? Tori—I mean Mom—said she never met them."

"I don't really remember them," Ethan says. He sits down on the rock and I walk over and sit next to him. "They weren't around when Chet died."

"So you were alone? In foster care?"

"Yeah, that was before Mom's place took me in."

"And then what happened? After Chet died?"

He's silent for a long time, but I don't rush him. And then after minutes of this silence, he says, "Where were your parents? When you were my age?"

"Well, my mom was... not well and then she..." I'm about to lie and say she got sick and died, but that's not a lie you tell a kid who's been through that already. "She killed herself. And then I was with my dad, and he was murdered by some bad people."

"Who?" Ethan says, looking up at me.

And here it is. The truth fucking staring me in the face. I can either admit it and get it over with now, or lie and let that lie fester for decades until he figures it out on his own.

I can't live with that lie. I can't live with any more lies. I've told too many of them already. So I say, "The Conrads. The Conrads killed him."

Ethan squints his eyes at me. "The people who adopted you?"

I nod.

"Jesus Christ, West. That's horrible."

And I can't help myself. I laugh pretty loud. He's like a thirty-year-old man in this little kid body. It's such a trip. "Yeah," I say. "They did a lot of bad stuff. Lotta bad stuff."

"And that's why Mom hates them?" he asks.

"Yup. And why she wants me to get rid of my last name and take the one I was born with."

"What?" Ethan says. "That would be like... me deciding to stop being Ethan Conrad and going backwards to become Ethan Wright again."

"Yeah, exactly how I feel about it."

"What's your real last name?"

"Conrad," I say, smiling. "What's yours?"

"Conrad," he says, smiling back. "Forever and ever and ever."

I ruffle his hair and say, "Yeah. But you know your mom..." I sigh. "She's real worried about you."

"I know," Ethan says. Just like that. *I know.* Like this is nothing in his world. "But she shouldn't worry too much."

"Why's that?" I ask.

"Because I'm OK now. I don't go out to steal food or medicine for Chet anymore. I just go out because... I like it. And I don't go very far. Not too far. Not like I used to before Mom found me. I just go short places. To see people I know and make sure they're OK."

Wow. I loved him before this conversation, but I love him even more now. I don't exactly know what kind of medicine he's talking about for his brother. But I'm gonna assume it was over-the-counter kinda stuff. Because if this kid was breaking into pharmacies for cancer drugs I might not know what to do with that.

So I say, "Ya know, there's this new invention called the smartphone."

He laughs.

"And the really cool thing about it is that you call people and ask them how they're doing. You don't even have to go over to their house to look into the windows or anything."

"Dad," he says.

"And not only that," I say, "but you can send little written messages called texts, if you don't feel like calling. People like texts. You can put little smiley faces in them and everything. Those are called emojis."

"Dad." He laughs again.

"My point is, Ethan, you can't go out at night. It's not safe. And it's driving your mother nuts with worry."

He sighs.

And I get all the things out of that sigh. He does it because... well, he likes to do it. And I get that. I used to catch lobsters and fish because I liked it too. But it was dangerous, and even though it was fun, and I learned a lot, and I became self-sufficient... "That's not how kids live, Ethan. Kids don't do those things because they need time to grow up. Kids need to have fun, but they need to have safe fun. Ya get me?"

He thinks about this for a long time, and I let him. We just sit there. And then, finally, he says, "I get you."

"So you'll stay home at night? And we'll get you a phone and put everyone's number in it? And you can call each one of them, every single night if you'd like, and ask them if they need anything."

He looks up at me and says, "What if they do need something?"

I shrug. "We'll get in the car and take care of it. Together."

"Promise?" he asks.

I nod. "Promise."

After another long silence he says, "OK. I'll do it your way."

"I love you, Ethan."

"I know," he says back.

"Hey," I say, deciding we've come to some kind of conclusion. "You wanna go catch some lobsters the real way?"

"Do we need gloves?" he asks. "Because I couldn't find any on the island last night."

"No," I say, feeling happier about everything. "Getting poked with spines is most of the fun."

"Battle scars," Ethan says.

"Battle scars," I say back.


Later, after we've caught our quota for the day and Ethan has moved on to fishing, I join Tori on the beach. She's got quite the setup down here. Giant umbrella, beach towel big enough to host a family of six, sunscreen, cooler with drinks and snacks... pretty much everything a family needs for a day at the beach.

"My hands sting like fuck," I say.

Tori lowers her sunglasses and smiles. "Best feeling in the world, right?"

"Best," I agree, sinking down beside her and stretching out my legs.

We sit there like that for a little bit, just watching Ethan's lean form silhouetted against the afternoon sun as he casts, and reels, and casts again. "He's OK," I say.

"I know," Tori says.

And I love this about her. That we have these conversations that are half words, half mind-reading.

"I love him so much," Tori says, her hand on her belly. Like she's subconsciously wondering if she will love the new baby more. Or less, for that matter.

But I know that's not really what's on her mind, so I don't even go there. "He loves you back," I say.

"I know that too."

"He wouldn't be here if he wasn't happy, Tori."

"What do you mean?" There's a little crack in her façade.

"I mean…" What do I mean? I think about it for a second because I feel like this is crucial. That the words need to be just right and there's no room for mistakes. "I mean… Ethan is like us."

"Explain," Tori says.

"We choose our path, we don't let it just happen to us. It's a force of will, and compromise, and maybe even a little bit of fate. But not really fate, because fate implies we don't control it, and we do. He's like us, Tori. We're together, not just because we're in love and it's a love that lasts forever through lifetimes, but because we want to be together. He's with us because… well, you didn't choose him and I didn't choose him. He's the one who chose us."

"You didn't choose your parents," she says.

But I'm ready for it. Ethan has clarified things for me in a way I would've never seen without him. "No, I didn't. They chose me. And it's not the same. Thank God, it's not the same. Because even though what they did was disgusting, unethical, and caused a lot of people a lot of pain… I had nothing to do with it. I didn't choose them, but I can't change the mark they left on me any more than you can change the mark your father left on you. Or Ethan can change the mark his childhood will leave on him. All we can do is admit our mistakes, try harder, do better, and live on. I'm a Conrad. I don't want to go backwards and be the kid I was before they took me in. And Ethan is a Conrad. So are you. We're not them, Tori. And this name has nothing to do with who we are. It's just a name, that's all. And we're gonna keep it. We're gonna do good things with our name."

"So Victoria Conrad," she says, trying out her new name.

"That's Mrs. Victoria Conrad to you."

She smiles and scoots closer to me, her hand on my stomach as mine wanders to hers. I think about the baby and wonder why I'm so calm about it.

One year ago I was Mr. Corporate. Power player. Master of my world.

I'm still him, just better. And fatherhood suits me, I decide. It's the best.

"Hey," I say. "You know what's so cool about having a kid?"

"The pregnancy sex?" she says, winking at me.

I have to stop and think about that for a minute. Jesus. "Yeah, that, for sure."

Tori laughs. "What's so cool about it?"

"You get to fix all the shit your parents fucked up."

Tori hugs me, wrapping her leg around mine in a possessive way that makes my heart swell. "You know what?"

"What?"

"It's funny how the worst day of your life can end up being the best day of your life. If we hadn't both been under those trees in front of the admin building that night at Brown, we'd never have met."

"Not true," I say. "Because I had my eye on you for weeks. You just scared the fuck out of me so I never approached you."

"Liar!" She laughs.

"Truth," I say. I look down at my soon-to-be wife and then kiss her. "But seeing you in your moment of weakness made me brave. And I guess that's a good lesson to learn. That it's our moments of weakness that define us. It's the challenges that mold us into who we become. The struggle makes the victory that much sweeter."

Tori sighs, looking out at Ethan as he reels in yet another fish. "He's gonna be just fine," she says.

"Better than fine."

"Just like us," she says.

"Just like us."

# PAX

There's bootprints in the spilled flour on the floor and several clumps of alfalfa hay strewn about.

My heart calms when I realize this is a setup.

That sneaky Miss Cookie. I'm gonna spank her ass cheeks red when I find her.

Which brings me to my next question. Where the fuck is she?

Hmmm… bootprints and hay. That can only mean one thing… she wants me to find her at the stable.

I grin, picturing myself throwing her down into a haystack, then fucking her wild from behind. "Game on, Miss Cookie," I say, leaving the kitchen house. She's teasing me, that's what she's doing. And I like it.

I have no idea where the fucking stable is on this island, so I stop by the house and find it empty. But out back by the pool, there's Five's girls dutifully taking their test.

Five is crazy and I'm not fixing this for him. He's just gotta come around to the idea. Besides, my cookie wants her nieces close to home. I'm taking her side on this.

"Hey," I call out to Rory. I don't know her that well, but she's my new sister, and I'm digging that whole aspect to this marriage stuff.

She shushes me, pointing to her girls, so I make a zipping motion at my lips and follow her inside the house. "Sorry," she says. "I just don't want them disturbed. This is the math part and it makes me nervous. Math was never my strong suit."

Which makes me laugh because Five, right? "I think they're fine," I say. "All I need is for you to point me in the direction of the stables. Your sister has a surprise waiting for me there."

I waggle my eyebrows, kinda forgetting she's a girl, but Rory just laughs. "Oh, yeah. She's full of surprises, all right. It's that way," Rory says, motioning over to a window that looks out on a winding path leading up a hill.

My eyes follow the trail and I feel tired already. I should not've gotten so drunk last night. "All the way to the top?" I ask.

"All the way to the top. It's got the best grass up there so they can graze."

"Of course it does," I say. I salute her, and start humming *I Wanna Be an Airborne Ranger* as I head out.

"And mind the stallion!" Rory calls. "We have two mares in heat!"

"I won't be fucking with him," I mutter. "Just your sister." Which makes me grin like a teenager.

By the time I'm halfway up the hill I'm sweating, cursing, too out of breath to sing, and *really* in need of some water.

I can see the barn and some ponies grazing in a nearby pasture. They come up to the fence lining the path and follow me like dogs. Cute fuckers. I'm trudging up the last hundred yards to the barn when I notice dirt bike tracks in fresh mud.

Which is weird because it hasn't rained and I haven't heard any dirt bikes on the island this morning. But just as I think that, I do hear one. Off in the distance over another ridge. Hmmm.

I keep going, hoping there's a fridge up here at the top or a hand-pump for a well. Or whatever it takes to get a drink. Because it's hot as hell now and I'm dehydrated as shit after drinking so much last night.

"Miss Cookie!" I call out, once I'm a little ways from the open barn doors. "Your detective is here!"

I expect some giggling or maybe a fake scream, but nothing. Just the clopping of hooves as the ponies trot back and forth near the fence, put off when I leave them behind.

That's when I smell gasoline.

Jesus, it's strong. I look around, trying to figure out where it's coming from and spy an old rag on the ground. There's more bootprints, more dirt bike-tracks, and on a open door leading out the back, some oily fingerprints.

"Cindy?" I call out. "Cinderella? You here, babe?"

Nothing.

Huh. There's no fridge that I can see, so I wander out of the barn and go looking for water. Out in the pasture I spy a hand-pump, so I jump the fence and slip between the two friendly ponies, who are now very interested in my pockets because they probably figure I've got treats.

I brush them aside, but they follow me all the way over to the water. I pump the handle a few times to get the flow going and I'm just about to bend down and drink when I hear a snort and the tell-tale pawing of a hoof.

I glance over my shoulder and see a beautiful golden pony about fifty yards away. "Hey there, pretty lady. You thirsty too?"

And that's when I realize… it's not a lady, it's a fella. And these two cute girls who've been following me are his mares. In heat.

I put my hand up because this *is* the universal gesture of surrender—for all species, as far as I know—and maybe I'm no horse expert, but I grew up on a breeding farm and if there's one thing I do know about them, it's that you do not fuck with a stallion. Even when he's only four feet tall.

"Cindy!" I yell. "If you're here, come save me from this tiny maniac!"

He charges me.

She never shows.

So I run.

I'm right at the fence, practically over it, when his teeth grab the flesh of my arm. I pull away instinctively, and hurl myself over the top rail. But that crazy little fucker still has a hold of my shirt, so I have to slip out of it to get the rest of the way over, and I land in a heap in the grass.

Golden Balls rears up like he's fucking king of the world, and snorts through his nose like he really wants to jump this fence and kill my ass.

Jesus.

I get up, flip him off, and then feel a whole lot better about shit since losing my shirt is probably a good thing. I'm hot as hell.

I glance over at the water, thirsty as all fuck, but then decide... I can wait. Obviously Cindy left me those dirt bike clues. Which means she's up wherever Five keeps them. I look over at the ridge where I heard the sound of riders a few minutes ago, and decide I might as well head in that direction.

I glance at the back of my arm and see teeth marks. Motherfucker bit me.

He and I exchange glares as I leave and I make a V with my fingers and point to my eyes, then him. "I'm watching you, Golden Balls."

I'm pretty sure the noise that comes out of his mouth is a laugh.

Fucking ponies.

The ridge doesn't look higher than the stable, but it is. Because I'm huffing my ass off as I walk up the slope. When I get to the top I expect to see a garage. A shed. Something that tells me, this is where we keep the dirt bikes.

Nothing but another fucking ridge.

So I trudge up that one too, and by this time, I might actually be dying of thirst. Like... *dying*.

When I get to the top, halle-fucking-lujah, there it is. There's two bikes parked outside. Little mini ones, like kids ride. But the door is wide open and I can hear music coming from inside. *Electric Worry*, by Clutch. Kind of an angry song if you ask me.

"Cindy?" I call out. But by this time, I've pretty much given up hope so I'm not surprised to find the place empty, save for a giant mud puddle in the center of the garage with something floating on top of it.

I'm so fucking thirsty I might get down on my hands and knees and slurp it up.

I grab the floating thing instead. It's one of those bobbing keychains people use for boats, and it's got two keys on it.

She's at the marina? Are you fucking kidding me right now? That's like... so far away. That's when I spy the sink in the corner.

Yes! Finally, some good luck!

171

I practically run over there, turn the water on and… see the sign above the faucet. *Non Potable Water—Do Not Drink!* 'Do not drink' has been underlined like a million times.

I consider how sick I'll get if I drink it anyway, and then decide I'm getting married tomorrow and I don't want the hassle this risk brings with it.

I look at the key in my hand and realize it's got a name on it. Louise.

Then I look at the two bikes out in front and smile. Because I think I have a key to one of those bikes and I'm gonna ride that fucker down to the marina and I'll be hydrated and kicking back on a boat in ten minutes.

I can handle ten more minutes.

I get on the bike, trying my best to ignore the fact that it was made for a five-year-old, and insert the key. There's a moment, right before I turn the ignition, that I think to myself, *It's broken. It's not gonna turn on. It's a setup. I'm gonna have to walk all the way back to the beach and I'm gonna die along the way.* But none of that happens. Because the engine turns over and I laugh. I laugh loud and I say, "Fuck, yes!"

I take off, still screaming, my knees all the way up to my elbows as I ride the tiny bike over the first ridge, then the second, and then I flip off Golden Balls as I whiz by.

Day made.

The hill looks a lot steeper going down than it did going up, and I give myself mental props for dealing so well, seeing as I'm still hungover, dehydrated, and on my way to a hell of a sunburn since I lost my shirt.

The path is winding and diverts away from the house towards the marina. I crane my neck, desperate for sight of the dock, and then I see it and whoop again.

I'm there. I'm fucking there, baby. "I'm coming, Miss Cookie! And I'm gonna spank you good for this wild-goose—"

The engine sputters.

I look down at the gas gauge and yell, "Nooooooo!"

The engine dies.

I coast as far as I can, but there's one more hill... and I just stop at the bottom and look up.

Defeated.

"You win!" I yell. I'm not sure what her point is to all this bullshit, but fuck it. I scream it anyway. "You win!"

The only answer I get is the sound of a boat leaving the marina and I swear to God, if Cindy just took off in a boat and expects me to follow her...

Well, I'll spank her twice as hard when I get a hold of her perfect round ass. Because I will catch her. She's not getting away.

In fact my energy is back, so I get off the stupid kid bike and push it up and over the last hill, and then I sit on it side-saddle style and coast down to the boat house.

Inside I hear... The Beach Boys. And what might be a fan going full speed. Then ice clinking in a glass, and I can't take it anymore. I get off the bike and burst through the door, ready to give Cinderella the spanking of her life, and then... and then I see her.

Naked. Sipping something cold and fruity. And holding another glass out for me. "Took you long enough, Detective. I'm practically drunk."

She's got on a hat, white sunglasses, and there's a mister in front of the fan, spritzing her lightly with water.

"You're a very bad girl, Miss Cookie." I growl out the words.

"I was kidnapped this morning," she says, lowering her sunglasses and opening her legs at the same time.

"By whom?" I ask, slightly less pissed off than I was a second ago.

"I'm not sure. I didn't get a good look at him, Detective. But he held me hostage in a cookie factory until he heard you were coming to save me."

"Let me guess, he took you up to the stable after that."

"He did," she coos.

"That fucking pony bit me!" I say, showing her the back of my arm.

"Oh, you poor baby. I'm gonna kiss it all better. In fact, I'm gonna kiss everything all better." She pokes her tongue against the inside of her cheek and I laugh.

"You dirty little bitch."

"And then," she says, still using her fake Miss Cookie voice, "then he took me up to the garage and was gonna tie me up and leave me there forever. Until he figured out you hadn't given up."

"I lost my shirt to that crazy midget horse. I'm fucking sunburned as all hell."

"I'm gonna rub sunscreen and lotion all over you, Detective. And I do mean... *all* over you."

Yeah, that sounds kinda fun. "And then that stupid bike was twelve sizes too small and I ran out of gas on the way down!"

"Don't worry," she whispers. "I've got enough fuel for both of us. I'll do all the work. I'll get on my hands and knees if I have to."

Fuck, yeah.

"And you got here in the nick of time."

"Why's that?" I ask, plopping down beside her. Her breasts are bare and her nipples hard and erect. Just like my cock.

"Because I was just about to give up hope and pleasure myself."

"Well," I say, looking away, then at her again. "You can still do that."

We both laugh this time.

But then she stops and her face gets all serious. Like she's worried about me. God, I hate it when she worries about me. "What's wrong with you?" she asks.

"Me? You're the crazy one who sent me on a wild-goose chase today! And where did you get all that blood in the kitchen house?"

"Oh, the cookie factory, you mean? Please, Paxton Vance. My family ran a haunted house for years. You don't think I know how to cook up some fake blood?"

"Right," I say, all my bullshit complaints fading fast. "Forgot about that."

"But seriously, Pax. What's the problem?"

"I don't have a problem."

"You got drunk last night. Really drunk last night. And you were singing an army song. Some might be wondering if you really wanted to marry me, or if you'd rather spend the rest of your life dealing with blood and danger."

"Ahh," I say, understanding now. "That's why you did this? You think I'm gonna miss it?"

"Will you?"

"Fuck, no," I say, scooting in close to her. "Fuck, no. I'm not worried about that."

"Then what?"

I sigh. Wondering if I should tell her what I did. Wondering what everyone will think of me when they find out.

"Pax, just tell me what's on your mind. You know I love you, right?"

"I know," I say.

"Then tell me what's wrong."

I sigh. Long and loud. "I did something bad, Cindy."

"How bad?" she asks.

I look up at her and shrug. "Pretty bad."

She pouts her lips. "Well, you've killed people before and didn't act this way. And I know you didn't cheat on me, so that can't be it."

"Cheat?" My laugh is so loud, it echoes off the ceiling. "Fuck, no, I didn't cheat."

"So what is it?"

"She's gonna hate me, Cindy."

"Who?"

"My mother."

"Why?"

"Because I did something she was one hundred percent totally against."

"I'm gonna punch you in the sunburn if you don't tell me what's going on right now."

"I invited my father to the wedding," I say. "And he'll be here tonight."

# CHAPTER TWENTY-FOUR

# OLLIE

Walking into the bike garage is like going home. All growing up this was the smell I knew best. Oil, and transmission fluid, and brake dust. I love it.

"So," I say, placing my hands on Kat's hips and swaying her a little. "Which bike should we fuck on?"

"Hmmm," she says, biting her fingernail. "That one?"

She points to an old motorcycle that looks like no one's ridden it in years. It's a Shrike Bike, one my father made some time before I was born probably. And it's got dusty ravens on the side.

Katya walks over to it and brushes off the gas tank with her fingers. "Shrike Rook," she says, reading the fancy painted script. "As in Rook, your aunt?"

I bend down to look at the old bike. "Hmmm, I've never seen this bike in person, but I've seen pictures of it. I think it was my mom's, but my dad said he wrecked it."

"Doesn't look wrecked to me." She laughs.

"No, me either. I bet he lied. To make sure she didn't ride it. I've heard stories about my mom in her younger days. She was wild. I can totally picture my dad smuggling it out here to Five's island to hide it away."

Katya lets her fingers linger on the tank, taking off more dust as she walks around it. "Why not just sell it?" she asks.

"Sell it? No way will my father ever sell this bike. It's special. This was the first bike he ever built. And I think

177

it had something to do with meeting my mom. But then...
I remember seeing it in one of the old *Shrike Bikes*
episodes. Back when he was doing the reality show. He
gave it to Rook, gave it a new paint job, and then she sold
it to my mom after Ronin told her she wasn't allowed to
ride it either."

Kat laughs. "You men. So worried about us." But
she's being playful and her fingertips are walking up my
button-down shirt, unbuttoning it as she goes.

"It's our job to worry," I say, loving her attention.
"For instance... I'm kinda worried about you right now."

"Me?" she says, looking up as she slides my shirt down
over my shoulders. "Why are you worried about me?"

I slip my hands inside her tank top and flatten my
palms against the curve of her waist. Loving how warm
she is. "Because I think you're sad. I think you're missing
your sister. And wishing your parents were here to see you
get married."

She nods, frowning for a moment. "I am missing
them. A whole lot, Oliver. But I'm trying not to think
about it. I'm trying to remember that I've got a whole new
set of friends to help me now. And Mariel is still here. So
I'm thankful for that. And your sisters—while a little scary
at times—will help."

"They'd do anything for you, Katya. Anything."

She nods, letting my shirt drop to the floor so she can
place her bare hands flat against the muscles of my chest.
"I know."

She says it like she's not sure. I'm sure, but I know
them. I know the fierce loyalty that glues us all together.
She's just seen a little bit of that loyalty so far. But one
day... one day she'll have a problem and need help. And

my sisters will come through for her in a way she can't even imagine right now. One day she'll understand.

Just not today, I guess. And that makes me sad. Because I want everything about this wedding to be perfect for her. I pick up my shirt, dust off the seat and tank of the bike, then lay her back on it.

She smiles, biting her lip. Because if she wants to fuck on a bike, she's gonna get fucked on a bike.

"Are you ready for more?" I ask, unable to stop the sly smile creeping up my face.

"Gimme more," she whispers, reaching for the button on my shorts. She pops it open and unzips the fly as I straddle the bike and maneuver my body over hers.

I lean down and kiss her lips, pulling her shirt up as I do it. My hands rest on her breasts, gently rolling them in my palms as my cock grows hard with want.

Her mouth is sweet and her tongue is cool. I kiss her gently, even though I know she's as tough as any girl I've ever met. I want to treat her carefully. The way she deserves to be treated. I want to erase all those bad years and replace them with goodness. Kindness and love.

"I never thought I'd find a woman like you."

"What kind of woman am I?"

"Perfect."

"No one's perfect, Oliver."

"Except you," I say. "You've got it all. Beauty. Intelligence. Common sense."

"I did fall in love with you," she says, smiling. "That might've been the best move yet."

"You falling in love with me was my luckiest break ever. You changed all my plans, Katya Shrike."

She giggles. "I can't believe we're getting married."

"We are," I say. "And tomorrow is gonna be the most beautiful day. And we're gonna spend forever and ever and ever connected to each other. Eternity," I say.

"Eternity, huh?" she asks.

I kiss her soft, sweet mouth again. Whispering, "Infinity, baby," right into her soul.

She grabs my cock and holds me. Tight. I close my eyes and let the throbbing take over. The want and longing I have for her is indescribable.

So we decide no more words are necessary.

I pull on her shorts and she lifts and bends her legs, pressing them together so I can pull them off. And then she opens for me, the inside of her knees rubbing against the outside of my thighs as I gaze down at her wet pussy.

She takes my cock out, pumping me slowly. I exhale, wanting more from her, just like she wants more from me. I want to do everything to her right now. Push my cock down her throat. In her pussy. Her ass. Eat her out, suck her clit, put my fingers inside her. Fuck her from behind, from above, from below.

And like she's reading my mind, she whispers, "We've got eternity, remember?"

I remember. So I go slow. I let her go slow too. I ease upward, position myself right in front of her entrance, and fill her up as I stare into her eyes.

She closes them for a moment. But just a moment. Like even she knows we've got so many more moments coming, but they will be perfect—too good to miss even a single one.

"You're my everything, Katya."

"And you're mine."

We don't fuck like animals. Or have the wildest sex of our lives. Maybe we'll do that later, maybe next year, or next lifetime, who knows? But this time right now, we stretch time out. We break all the rules of physics as we move together like we're just a single person now. Like Oliver and Katya cannot exist alone ever again.

And I hear that song in my head. Our song. *She gives me more... and more... and more...*

We come together.

As one.

Because that's the only way we can possibly exist.


Later, after we pull ourselves apart, we gas up the two adult-sized dirt bikes and head out to the stables for the next leg of our perfect day. The sun is shining and the temperature is rising, and honestly, everything about this day is bliss.

Cindy goes galloping past us on a pony as we head down, and I look over my shoulder to see if she wants us to stop and talk, but she's already disappeared around a bend in the road.

No idea what my baby sister is up to, but she's not with Pax, so fuck it. That, at least, makes me happy.

When we get to the stables, we saddle up an old draft horse and ride double down to the marina. I haven't ridden double since I was a little kid, and I definitely don't remember loving it this much. But Katya, who it turns out has never ridden before, presses herself into my back as I lead us down the hill. She rests her chin on my shoulder, and wraps her arms around my middle, and we rock with the rhythm of a swaying back and the music of clopping hooves. She talks about the island, and the wedding, and her dress—which she is so excited to try on later tonight and see what alterations Rory has made.

I hang on every word. I can't get enough of her sweet voice in my ear. Her soft breath ruffling the tiny hairs of my neck.

We leave the horse in a pasture to graze and decide we'd rather snorkel than dive—because who has time for diving gear? And neither of us want to be that covered up. Her bikini is a light tangerine color, and her hair is up in some makeshift bun, and she's got dirt and dust from the old bike smeared across her cheek before we dive in, but I think she's never looked more beautiful. So I burn that image of her in my mind, and we hold hands and jump off the dock, and then we swim over the secret world that lives below the surface and... and it's perfect.

This island is paradise and I wish we could stay here forever and never go back to real life. Like Five and Rory did. Raise a little family out here on the beach and pretend we're the only two people on the planet.

When we're tired and we've seen all the fish, we drag ourselves out of the water, feeling heavy and sedated. And we take the boat over to the little sandy island and plop down on a blanket under a palm tree shaped like an umbrella. I feed her muffins from the picnic we packed, and we drink bottles of exotic water, and she falls asleep in my arms once or twice, or maybe a couple dozen times.

That's where we are now. Living in bliss.

"Should we go back?" she asks me, her words low, and throaty, and filled with satisfaction. "Won't your family be here soon?"

"Sure," I say. "We can. But man, this is the life, right?"

"It's the best getaway ever," she agrees. "I'd like to come back some day. When life gets to be too much, this is where we should come."

"I could live here," I say, my eyes still closed. "It's fucking perfect."

"Could you really, though?" she asks.

"Could I really what?"

"Live here."

"Hell, yes." I laugh.

"Wouldn't you get bored?" she asks.

"Bored? Nah, there's so much do."

"Yeah," she agrees. "But we did it all, right? I mean, realistically, what more is there to do here? We rode the bikes, the horse, saw the reef, and rested on the most perfect island. But there's more to life than downtime, right?" She props herself up on one elbow and smiles at me. "Like shopping."

I laugh. "Yeah, I mean, the grocery store is kinda far."

"So far! And what if you wanted like... a bubble bath? And you're out of bubbles. You'd have to plan your bubble baths. Or what if you wanted to see a movie? Not a DVD, but a movie?"

"Five has a satellite," I say. "Pay-per-view, I guess."

"So I guess date nights are out?"

"I guess," I say, frowning. "But this is a pretty good date, don't you think?"

"The best," Kat says, leaning over to kiss my lips. "The very best date ever. But..." She hesitates. "Forget about dates, then. What if we got sick? Or one of us got hurt? It's a long helicopter ride to Nassau, and I'm not entirely sure what kind of hospitals they have there, but I'd bet we'd have to go to Miami if something really went wrong. That's kinda scary, right?"

"Yeah," I say, thinking it over.

"And your family would be so far away. It's like five hours by plane. So far. Wouldn't you miss them?"

"I would," I admit. "Call me a mama's boy if you want, but I like living close to my parents. And my sisters, crazy as they are."

"So don't you ever wonder if…"

She's silent for a few seconds. And when she doesn't add to that, I ask, "Wonder what?"

"Don't you ever wonder if Rory doesn't think of this place more as a… prison? Than a paradise?"

"What?" I laugh. "No. She's with Five."

"And that's all she needs?"

"Yeah," I say. "They're like—"

"Soulmates. I know. You told me that already. And I don't want you to take this the wrong way, Oliver, because you and I are soulmates too, but if I had to live on this island for so many years, with no chance to have my own life apart from yours, I'd go crazy. Absolutely crazy."

I don't know what to say to that. At first I'm kinda pissed off. But she makes sense, so I dial down my anger and stew in it for a little bit.

"I'm just saying that… well, you know Pax didn't steal Cindy from you. It was Five who stole Rory. It's Five you're really mad at."

"No," I say, not laughing at all now.

"Maybe not," she says, standing up and brushing sand off her body. I watch her put her bikini back on, then tie the strings of her top when she turns her back to me. "Maybe I'm totally wrong about that." She smiles and extends her hand. I take it and she pulls me to my feet. "But then again, maybe I'm not."

I think about that the whole way back to the island.

Am I mad at Five? Am I… what do they call it? Transferring my anger at losing Rory onto Pax for falling in love with Cindy?

I pull the boat up to the dock and Kat jumps out to tie it up. She talks about stuff as we make our way back to the bungalow to shower, change, and get ready for the parents to arrive.

But I can't stop thinking about it now.

Is Rory happy? Is this paradise? Or is this just a prison Five's locked her in?

Is she Rapunzel? Is this island just another tower made to hold a princess?

Has she been miserable all this time? Has she been waiting for one of us to save her? Is this why she's got her twins testing? While everyone's here? So they will take up her fight and convince Five to let her leave?

I feel sick.

Utterly sick.

# CHAPTER TWENTY-FIVE

# FIVE

We linger on the grotto rock for a while, eyes closed and breathing slow. My hand wanders down her stomach, fingertips fluttering over her belly button.

I can't see her smile when I do that, but I know it's there. I know her so well.

"What's on your mind?" she asks.

And she knows me too.

"Just life and how it's changing. How the girls are growing up and how I don't want that to happen."

"All kids grow up, Five."

"I know. But I'm not ready for it."

"They need to see the world."

"I agree," I say. "But I'm not convinced that the world needs to see them."

She rolls over on her side, sighing heavily. Her fingertips find my stomach, the same way mine found hers. She tickles me as she brushes her nails lightly up and down my skin. "They're ready. And so am I."

Which is the part I'm worried about, right? I'm still content and happy to be out here in paradise with them, and they're moving on.

"Are you tired of me?" I ask her.

"What?" She laughs out the word. "Don't be ridiculous. I'm more in love with you today than I was yesterday. And yesterday I was more in love with you than

I was the day before. That's how it's always been. Our love just… grows. And you can't stop it."

"Like the girls," I say.

This time I see her smile. Because she's looking right at me. "Yeah, like them too."

We lie there in silence for a few more minutes. The grotto is humid and hot, since the sun and the day, like our love and our girls, can't be stopped either. But the mist from the waterfall keeps us cool.

"I bet they're done by now," Rory says.

"Probably," I say, unable to stop the sadness in my voice.

"Let's go back and I'll make us all lunch. I've got a ton of work to do before tonight. I want to get the pool area set up for the parents and make sure dinner's on track. Plus, I have to find Katya and get her to try on her dress."

"Kat and Oliver are on a date day. They probably won't be back until later." I say it as a last-ditch effort to keep her here with me. Just me. Just her.

But it doesn't work. She says, "That's OK. I've got to check on the baking and decorations too. And find Louise and Mathilda and make them take a bath before the party."

I get up without comment. Because I can't keep her here all day. She's right, there's so much to do. I hold out my hand and she takes it so I can pull her to her feet. We stand there, staring at each other for a few seconds. And then she cups my face with both her hands and kisses me on the lips. "You're OK, Five. I promise. You're gonna live through this."

"It's just moving so fast all of a sudden."

"It's not," she says. "It's moving at just the right pace."

She waits to see if I'll keep the discussion going, but I don't. So she grabs my hand, leads me over to the waterfall, and we dive in together.

When we resurface on the other side the real world is back.

We swim over to the edge of the lake and drag ourselves out of the water, sopping wet. And then we walk home. Silent. Holding hands. Thinking about two totally different versions of the future.

When we get back to the pool, the twins are swimming. Obviously the test is over. I look around for the sealed envelope I know they're in, but all evidence of the test-taking is gone. No pads of scratch paper, no pencils, no Ming, either.

Rory jumps in the pool with the girls and they splash and play a little as I settle into a chair under the shade of the palapa.

I need to find Mysterious. I'm not giving up on this plan of mine just yet. But I don't want to leave them. So I watch a little longer. Then a little longer still. Until Rory says, "Have you seen your sisters?" to the twins, which gets my attention, because they've been off doing stuff all day.

"They came back a little while ago covered in mud," Ana says.

"Mud!" Rory exclaims. "Jesus! Five, can you go find them and get them cleaned up?"

"Sure," I say. Because it gives me the perfect excuse to find Pax. "Hey," I call out to the girls. "Have you seen Paxton? Or Cindy?"

"Nope," they both shout back at the same time. Twinning. And that makes me smile and forget that they're about to leave me behind and never look back. So I feel a little better as I say, "I'll see ya later."

"Dinner's at eight!" Rory calls. "And the parents should all start arriving around seven. Don't be late!"

"I'll be there!" I say. She blows me a wet kiss from the water and I do that stupid thing where you catch it in the air and slap it on your cheek. Which makes my girls all erupt in laughter.

I laugh too, but then when I turn and walk down the path leading to the house, the smile fades.

*This shit is happening, Five Aston. They're growing up. And Mr. Mysterious is your last fucking chance to change it.*

I look all over the place for Mysterious. He's not in his bungalow, or down at the beach, or at the kitchen house where I sent him last. I'm just about to go up to the stables to see if he's up that way when Mathilda and Louise appear from the jungle looking like they rolled in the mud and then hosed themselves off, but didn't do a very good job at it.

"What the… what have you two been up to?"

"Nothing," they say together. Hands behind their backs, feet fidgeting.

But this isn't twinning, like Ana and Isa. This is a lie. They do that, these little ones. They lie… and that's when I hear the squealing. "What have you got behind your back?" I ask them.

"Nothing," they say again.

"Girls," I say, putting on my stern father face. "Stop lying and show me what's behind your back."

They look at each other, then shrug like it's inevitable. Louise scrambles behind Mathilda, and then they both produce… a piglet.

I cover my mouth so they can't see me laugh, take a moment to gather myself back into parent mode, and then say, "Where did you get that pig?"

"The beach," Mathilda says.

"Didn't we discuss this, ladies? I told you, those pigs are off limits. You have to leave them be. And you'd better not have been feeding them."

They just stare at me with blank poker faces. Which means they sure as fuck did feed them. "Where is this pig's mother?" I ask.

"She abandoned it," Mathilda says. "It was starving, Daddy."

Yup. This is not good. "How did you get that pig?"

"We fed it mangos," Louise says. "And bananas." She makes a pouty face that usually works to defuse my anger.

But it's not working now. "I've told you a hundred times we can't feed them or they won't stop coming around looking for food."

"We're sorry," Mathilda says. "We won't do it again. But we had to save him, Daddy. We just had to."

If I had more time I'd punish them. But I don't. And they need to get ready for the party. So I just do basic dad duty instead. "Are you hurt?" I ask, turning Louise around to look her over. She's wet, and got mud all over her hair, but seemingly unharmed. "You can't mess with those pigs when they have babies, girls. You know better and I'm not happy with you. You should've asked before you went off and did dangerous things—"

"We didn't do it," Louise says.

"What?" I ask, looking at Mathilda. "What's she talking about?"

"Mr. Romantic," Mathilda says, like this explains everything.

191

"What's Nolan have to do with this?"

"We bribed him into catching our pig," Mathilda explains.

"Can we keep him, Daddy?" Louise says, looking up at me with those wide blue eyes of hers. "Please?" she begs, grabbing both my hands and jumping up and down.

"Please, please, please," Mathilda says.

"He's gonna die, Daddy," Louise continues. "If we don't keep him, and feed him, and give him a bed, he's gonna die."

"We can't let him die, Daddy!" Mathilda says, turning on the tears. "We just can't!"

I roll my eyes. My girls are spectacular actresses. They really should go into theatre.

*You don't have a theatre on the island,* that nagging voice in my head says. *So they'll never go into theatre.*

I shut that down and run all the reasons why we can't keep a wild pig as a pet. It might have diseases. Swine flu, for instance. Or it might grow up huge and attack us. I try to think up a few more, just to build a better case, but the pig snorts and draws my attention down to his pudgy belly, which is right side up as he lies in Mathilda's arms, half asleep and looking like a stuffed toy.

I sigh.

"We'll take really good care of him, Daddy!" Louise says.

"You'll never have to feed him, or watch him, or anything!" Mathilda adds.

But they're both wearing those smiles. You know the ones… the ones kids wear when they know they're gonna win this battle.

So I say, "Baths. Now. All of you. Including that pig."

"Yes!" they both squeal, which wakes the snoozing pig up and makes him squeal with them.

"And put on your pretty clothes. Grandma and Grandpa are coming tonight with all your aunts and cousins."

"We will!" they call out, already running off.

I don't know how Rory is gonna feel about a pet pig, but at least the little girls are still happy about living on the island. You can't catch and keep wild piglets in Colorado, can                                                     you? So that lifts my spirits. Mathilda and Louise will both be on my side when I have to put my foot down about Ana and Isa leaving.

Because we'd all have to leave if they leave. I can't send my girls out into the world alone. What kind of father would I be if I did that? If they leave, we all leave. And if we all leave... paradise is lost.

I follow the girls back to the house, preoccupied with how our lives seem to be changing so suddenly, when I bump into West, Tori, and Ethan.

"Hey," I say, as the three of them walk up the path towards me. "Whatcha got there?" I ask.

"Fish!" Ethan says, holding up his catch for the day.

"Holy..." And then I laugh. "What are you doing? Feeding the entire wedding party with that catch?" All three of them have nets filled with fish, not to mention a cooler filled with lobsters.

"Looks that way," West says, ruffling his boy's hair.

"Here," I say, taking Tori's net. "We'll take them to the kitchen. Have you seen Paxton anywhere?" I ask, remembering what my mission was before I bumped into the pig problem.

"I think I saw him with Cindy down by the boathouse about an hour ago," Tori says. "But I'm pretty sure they're gone now."

"Great," I say as we walk up to the kitchen house. That means he doesn't need my help in Cindy's little scavenger hunt. Which also means he's probably not gonna help me steal those tests.

"What time's dinner?" West asks. "We need to clean up."

"I think everyone starts arriving around seven and dinner's at eight. Just clean up and head to the pool. Everyone will be there by then and we can have a drink." I'm pretty sure Tori hates me after all that shit that went down last year, but it never hurts to patch things up. Especially when Ariel is coming tonight. Tori and Ariel are best friends now, from what Oliver's told me. And it never hurts to have a backup when it comes to Ariel Shrike. She's gonna have something to say about this whole lie we've been living. Oliver might've taken it all in stride, but Ariel? No way.

We hand the fish and lobster off to the catering staff flown in from Nassau for the wedding, and then go our separate ways.

Them to their bungalow, I presume. Me to try to catch Mysterious alone before dinner. Maybe he can grab those tests tonight? Replace them with blank pages or something?

I'm thinking that's a very good idea when I get to their place, and I'm just about to knock when I hear Cindy say, "Fuck me, Detective," from an open window.

My knuckles stop the knock just in time. I could interrupt them, but something tells me Mr. Mysterious takes his sex as seriously as he takes his drink. So even though I'm dying to wrap this plan up and tie it up in a bow, I back off and head home.

Four kittens attack me at the door and I'm cursing Mathilda and Louise under my breath. They're supposed to be taking care of them, not letting them run loose on the island all day. And when Rory finds out I let them keep that pig…

"There you are!" Rory says, opening the door. "Come on. Hurry up. Everyone's gonna be here soon. We gotta get cleaned up."

After that time rushes by with no sympathy for all the things we need to get done and before I know it, our families are landing out on the helipad and people are arriving at the marina, and I'm looking around for my two little princesses, because they disappeared about an hour ago and Rory put me in charge of keeping track of them.

I go out to the play house to see if they're there and walk in on… a tea party. But not your typical tea party.

I cover my hand to stifle a laugh when I see Nolan sitting on top of a fuzzy pink pillow in a tiny white chair. "What the hell?"

"Hey, Five," Nolan says, cool as ever. "Just having a little tea with your girls." He brings a tiny tea cup to his lips and sips.

"Are you pointing your pinky finger?" I ask. "I need a picture of this."

"Is it time, Daddy?" Louise says, jumping up from her seat.

"It's time," I say, pointing to the ceiling of the play house. "Hear the helicopters? Everyone's here. Come on, we gotta go."

"I'll take them," Ivy says, standing up from her place at the table with Bronte in her arms. "I can't wait to see my parents."

I herd the girls out after Ivy and then I turn to Nolan. "I hear you caught a pig for my girls today."

Nolan points to the corner where said pig is sleeping on top of a pink velvet cushion. "You mean that pig?"

"They very one," I say. "And what the fuck happened to your head?"

Nolan gingerly touches the giant lump near his ear. "Louise doesn't exactly have the best aim. She hit me with a rock."

"She *what*?"

"Well, in her defense, she was aiming for the daddy pig."

It suddenly occurs to me that I have no idea what my kids were up to today. And Rory is gonna kill me when she finds out how this pig thing went down. "What the hell were you thinking, Romantic?"

"Hey, they offered me a deal. I couldn't pass it up."

I want to argue with him, tell him about the nuisance these pigs are if you feed them. Smack him in the head, right on that lump the size of an egg, and call him an idiot. But I hear more helicopters arriving and decide it'll have to wait. "Come on, everyone's here. We can settle this later."

Back up at the house there are dozens of people crowded around the pool where we're having the party. I spy Spencer and Veronica laughing and joking with my mom and dad, then look the other way and see all Rory's sisters hugging her and jumping up and down. All except Ariel. I look for her because I know she's gonna be a problem. But she's not here. Did she stay home? Was she so pissed off we left her out of the plan to save Rory that she refused to come?

Nah. She has to be here somewhere.

"Hey," Katya says, coming up to me as I make my way around the pool, heading towards Rory so I can say hi to my sisters, Sasha, Kate, and Wendy.

"Hey," I say to Katya. I don't know her very well. I wasn't part of all that shit that went down with Oliver last year. I was too worried about making sure no one got wind of Rory and our little island paradise.

"Have you seen Oliver?" she asks.

"No, why?"

"I was just with him like twenty minutes ago when everyone got here, but now he's disappeared."

"I'm sure he's here somewhere, Kat. Just lost in the crowd."

"OK." She sighs. "I'll keep looking."

Katya walks off, looking a little bit lost in the crowd of mostly strangers. She's met the Shrikes—hell, she eats Sunday dinner over there every weekend back home. But it's gotta be intimidating, right? All those people in one place. So tight. So close. So connected.

And she has no one but Oliver.

I feel bad for her.

I think Rory does too because she's been going out of her way to make Kat happy, even altering her dress for her last-minute to make her wedding day perfect.

I look around for Oliver again because two Shrikes missing is probably not a good thing. I see Nolan and his mother talking with the Rockwells. Pastor Rockwell looks like he's giving the infamous Mr. Romantic the third degree about his granddaughter, while Mrs. Rockwell holds Bronte and showers her with kisses. Poor Nolan. No one ever cuts that guy a break. Not even me.

I see Mysterious and Mariel. Kat's over there now, probably asking the two of them if they've seen Oliver. Mysterious looks oddly... uncomfortable. He catches my eye and shakes his head like something's about to go really wrong. I decide to head over there and investigate, when a hand slaps over my mouth and I'm pulled into the bushes.

"I need to have a word with you, Five Aston," Oliver hisses in my ear as he throws me aside.

"What the fuck are you doing?" I ask, stumbling. When I turn around, straightening out my shirt, I find a very pissed-off Oliver Shrike and his equally terrifying sister, Ariel. They both stand, feet shoulder-width apart, arms crossed, and faces that tell me... yup. This is the freak-out I've been expecting all along.

"You stole my fucking sister," Oliver says.

"Mine too," Ariel adds.

"And if you think we're gonna let you keep her prisoner out here in the middle of the ocean one more second, you're sadly mistaken, *brother*."

I actually laugh. "What the fuck are you talking about? Keep her prisoner?"

"Don't play with us," Ariel says. "We know you talked Rory into doing this. She doesn't want to be here. She wants to be home with us. And that's why she's got her girls taking that test."

"*Our* girls," I correct her, my temper rising.

"She wants out, Five. And you won't let her leave," Oliver says.

"And we're taking her with us," Ariel snarls. "I don't even think she should marry you tomorrow."

"Whoa," I say, hands up. "What the hell are you two talking about? Of course Rory wants to be here."

"No," Oliver says, shaking his head. "She doesn't, Five. And it makes me sick to think you've been holding her here with my nieces all these years."

I start to explain that's not how it is when Ariel takes a swing at me and hits me right in the fucking eye.

"Bastard!" she yells.

And then Ollie is there, pulling her off me, and I elbow him—not entirely by accident—right in the lip.

"What the fuck, Ariel?" Rory is there, then when I look over my shoulder, everyone is there. Crowding in to see us. "What's going on here?"

I dab a finger on my eye and find it already swelling up. "They think I'm keeping you prisoner out here," I say.

"He's not keeping me prisoner, Ollie," Rory says. And then she glares at Ariel. "And I cannot believe you hit him in the eye the night before our wedding. What's wrong with you two?"

"Us?" Ariel says. She's flaming mad. No one wants to mess with Ariel Shrike when she's angry.

Except Princess Shrike. Because she stands in front of me and points her finger at both their faces. "Let me make this very clear. I get that you're my siblings, but this man," she says, tugging on my arm, "and these girls," she says, motioning to our princesses, "they're my family now. And you do not get to come into my house and start shit with my family."

"Do you really want to be here?" Oliver says. "Because if you ask me, a woman who wants to be here wouldn't set up secret tests for her children so she can use school as a reason to get them off the island."

The four of us just stand there looking at each other.

But it's the silence that lingers in the aftermath of his accusation that kills me.

I turn to Rory. "Is that why you did it?" I ask. "To… *escape?*"

"No," Rory says. "They have no idea what they're talking about."

"Then why did you keep it secret?" I ask. My heart might be breaking right now. If she's felt this way… how long has she felt this way?

"Five…" She stops. Like she's not sure what to say.

"Rory," I say. "Do you think I'm keeping you prisoner?"

"Yes," Oliver says.

But Rory turns on him, furious. "Shut your mouth, Oliver Shrike. Right now." She's pointing her finger at him and it's shaking with anger. "You have no idea what we've dealt with over the past twenty years. None. Do you remember that day at Brown when you thought you saw me in a crowd?"

"That was you!" Ollie says. "I knew that was you!"

"Yes, it was me. I was there because we got word that something might be going down and you might be involved. And even though Five said no, I did it anyway. I risked my entire family to try to stop it. And do you know why I did that?"

Oliver shrugs. "Because you're a fucking Shrike and you just take what you want?"

I hear her father laughing somewhere behind us.

"Yes," Rory says. "That's exactly why. And do you know what it taught me when all that bullshit was over?"

This time she's talking to Ariel, who just stands there and has the good sense to say nothing. You really do not want to mess with my wife when she's mad. "It taught me," Rory continues, "that this man," she says, grabbing my arm in a tight hold, "knows what the fuck he's talking about when it comes to keeping us safe. That's why I'm here, Oliver. Not because someone is forcing me. So you'd better back the fuck off and keep your face out of my business."

Everyone. Is. Silent.

And I have to cup a hand over my mouth to stop the laugh.

That's when Rory turns on me. "And you," she says, her shaking finger pointed in my direction now. "Paxton told me what you were planning. How could you even think of sabotaging those tests?"

I find Paxton in the crowd and glare at him.

"Don't blame him," Rory says. "He's not the idiot who came up with that stupid idea. He's the one who had the good sense not to go through with it."

I look at Oliver, who is shaking his head at me. I appreciate the warning, but I don't need it. I know Rory Shrike better than anyone on this planet and when she's fed up, she's fed up. We're all on her shit list tonight.

"I just..." I sigh. Long and loud. "I just don't want us to leave. I love it here. We've had a good, safe life, Rory."

"Life isn't always about being safe, Five." Her voice is soft now. And she moves in close to me and takes my face in her hands. "I miss my family. I want to see my mountains again. I want to swim in my mom and dad's pool and have sex with you in the grotto like we did that one day. I want to see the river again. Listen to it at night. And have coffee at the theater. I want to walk downtown and know that on every corner, there's someone nearby I can trust. Talk to. Have fun with. Cry with. I need my people back, Five. And our girls going off to school isn't an excuse to make you see things my way. It's just... what's best now."

I deflate. Just... deflate. "I didn't know," I say, looking at Oliver and Ariel. "I didn't know she wanted this so bad."

"Five," Rory says, still holding my face. "I haven't been pretending to love it here. I do love it here. But I'm allowed to love more than one place in the world. We did it," she says. "We won. And now we need to move on and win at something else."

I'm just about to respond when the little piglet shoots out from the bushes squealing. The girls have him dressed up in a pink ruffle tutu, and everyone takes this moment to laugh at our perfectly timed comic relief.

"What the hell?" Rory says, looking at the ass-end of the piglet as it scurries away.

"I'll have to tell you all about it later," I say.

And that's when we all turn our heads to stare at the jungle where the pig just emerged. There's a thundering sound, like a herd of horses galloping across the prairie.

A pack of wild pigs bursts through the foliage and swine hell breaks loose.

"Run!" Nolan says. "Run!"

The whole crowd squeals with the pigs as they trample the party. Trays of seafood go flying as the pigs root through everything. Louise starts hurling mangos and bananas at them. Ethan jumps up on a table and begins throwing lobster claws, while Mathilda picks up the piglet and takes off. I'm dragging Rory to the other side of the pool to get away from the stampede, yelling "Get over here, you crazy shits!" to my kids.

Louise and Mathilda are wild with laughter and intent on protecting their new pet.

That's when Nolan gets hit in the head with a mango, and I look just in time to see Louise laughing at her bad aim.

Then, as if things couldn't get any wilder, a bunch of spotlights appear in the sky and the sound of helicopters fills our ears.

"What the hell is happening?" Rory yells over the spinning rotors.

I just shake my head. I have no clue.

Then a guy I've seen in movies, but never in person, bursts into the pool area, yelling, "Shit! Shit! Shit! Hide! It's the paparazzi! They followed me here!"

The pigs, scared away by Louise and Ethan hurling food at them, or maybe the deafening sound of a swarm of helicopters as they circle around our island sanctuary, leave as quick as they came and...

Katya appears wearing a tattered wedding dress, a kitten hanging off it, crying her eyes out as she tries to swat it away. "The attacked me!" she wails. "They attacked me and they ruined my dress!"

# CHAPTER TWENTY-SIX

# MAC

Everything that happens next is a blur. Oliver rushes to Katya, trying to understand why she's got a pack of kittens running around her feet. Mariel is yelling, "Who the hell invited you to this wedding?" to Charles Vance, who just stands there stunned in his ten-thousand-dollar suit with his hands up, like Mariel's got a gun on him. The Shrike women all circle around Katya and Oliver, horrified expressions on their faces at the tattered remains of her dress. The piglet in a tutu goes wild, squealing loose from Louise's arms, and then does a flip in the air and lands on his feet, scurrying away. All five children go racing after him, which results in an upended table of lobster as he scampers onto a chair, leaps for the table, and doesn't quite make it. The next thing I hear is a splash, and when I turn my head, there's Mrs. Rockwell in the pool, her dress floating up around her like an unfolding parachute.

I see this in perfect clarity, because overhead there are at least six helicopters circling with spotlights.

The paparazzi just got it all on video.

Five roars, "Who the fuck invited the movie star to my island?" And then he looks at Pax, and Pax puts his hands up, just like his father did. And then Pax just turns and runs, Five chasing after him into the jungle.

I look at Ellie. She's doing her best to understand what happened too. And then she looks at me and we can't help it. We laugh. We laugh like idiots.

Nolan hands baby Bronte to Ivy, who is trying to calm her father down, and then Nolan jumps into the pool to rescue his new mother-in-law. But at the same time, Mariel takes a swing at Charles, which hits him square in the jaw, and he goes stumbling backwards into the pool as well, crashing into Nolan's mother, who crashes into Nolan, who sinks below the surface.

That's when the herd of pigs reappears.

Everyone screams and runs. People are flying off in all directions as the pigs root around in the remnants of the seafood platter that is now on the pool deck.

Then I see West trying to drag Ethan off the back of the biggest pig, because he thinks he's gonna ride it like a bull, and Tori is standing there, holding her hair with both hands, like this can't be happening.

"This can't be happening," Ellie says.

"Oh, it's happening," I say. "And this is fucking spectacular."

We laugh again, mostly because it's just funny. But also because we're just bystanders to the unfolding chaos.

Now the kittens are climbing up Oliver's pant leg and he's jumping around trying to shake them off, looking like a girl trying to swat off a spider. Then Ariel Shrike gets pelted in the stomach with a lobster claw, hurled by Mathilda who is chasing down a pig, and Ariel decides she's had enough and tackles the pig and knocks it into the pool, totally ruining Nolan's attempt to save his mother-in-law, and he goes under again.

Then all the pigs are in the pool. I'm not sure if they've got some kinda pact that if one pig goes in the water they all go in, but that's what it looks like to me. Because the chaos settles down as all the pigs do the doggie paddle around Charles, and it looks a little bit like a synchronized swimming performance. Charles is now yelling back at Mariel. "You're crazy!" he's screaming.

That's when the little tutu pig squeals. Everyone turns to look at the desert table where the piglet is happily grunting as he roots deep into the center of tonight's cake, stuffing his little piggy face.

Ellie and I laugh again.

Because this whole thing is nuts.

"This is the best wedding ever," Ellie sighs, grabbing onto my arm and leaning against me.

I hold her close as people come back to their senses. All the kittens are scooped up, the pigs are left alone to enjoy the pool, Mrs. Rockwell and Nolan's mother get dragged out of the water. Mariel decides to help Charles escape his wet pig prison, and gives him a hand up. Veronica and her bombshell daughters usher Katya into the house to figure out what to do about the dress. Ford Aston comes out of the jungle leading Five with a strong grip on his arm, Paxton following at a safe distance, trying to stop the bleeding from his nose by holding the cuff of his suit coat against it. West and Tori have finally gotten Ethan to calm down, and Spencer Shrike has his granddaughters all herded under the palapa and is giving them a stern talking-to about wild pigs.

I look up at the helicopters and I can almost hear the paparazzi laughing. Then I glance over at Ellie and grin. "The most perfect wedding ever. And I guess Five is just gonna have to come clean with the world about his secret life out here in paradise. Because it's totally gonna be on the news by tomorrow."

207

# CHAPTER TWENTY-SEVEN

# NOLAN

By the time everything settles down it's late. The pigs were shooed away, the food was cleaned up, and either the helicopters ran out of fuel or the paparazzi figured they got more than enough footage to satisfy the entire world for the next week, because they disappeared too.

Mariel and Charles came to some kind of agreement. My mother laughed the whole thing off like this is just what she expected to happen, while Ivy's parents didn't take it so well. I haven't seen them since they disappeared back to their bungalow to change.

I'm pretty sure Pastor Rockwell hates my guts even more now.

Every Shrike woman is in Rory's house trying to fix Katya's dress. Ivy wanted to help, and she did go over there, but she came back to our bungalow a little while ago because she said, "They've got this."

I'm gonna assume those Shrike women know what they're doing—because, well, they always seem to know what they're doing—so we put Bronte down for sleep and now we're just having a glass of wine to relax. Ivy's got her feet in my lap and she's talking about tomorrow. How everything went wrong tonight, so tomorrow will go off without a hitch.

But... we're the Misters, so you never know. Today was a disaster as far as I'm concerned. All I wanted was some time alone with my wife and I feel like I spent this day with everyone but my wife. Now it's almost midnight and she's probably just ready for sleep.

There's a knock at our door and Ivy jumps up, saying, "I'll get it," before I can even set my wine down. Great. There goes my last chance at some *us* time.

"Oh, look who it is!" Ivy exclaims. "Mac and Ellie! Come in!"

I get up to say hi, wondering why Ivy is so damn excited about seeing them at midnight. "Hey, what's up?" I ask Mac. "Whadda day, huh?"

"Fuckin' perfect day," he says back.

"So, uh… what can we do for you?"

"Well," Ellie says. "You can let us take it from here."

"Take what from where?" I ask.

"Babysitting," Ellie says, smiling up at Mac. "We're here to babysit for you guys."

"You know," Ivy says. "So we can go have that date you promised me?"

"What?" I ask, unable to stop my smile.

"We're going on a date today, Mr. Romantic. It's not midnight yet, so as long as we leave in the next seven minutes, you're gonna be able to keep that promise."

"But I thought…" I nod my head at Ellie.

"Oh, please," Ellie says. "I'm happy to watch Bronte. I just overreacted and Mac went overboard with that request. Any time you guys need a sitter, you call me first, understand?"

I look at Ivy and grin. "We get to go out… alone?"

"Alone," Ivy says back. "Come on." She takes my hand and pulls me out the door, calling over her shoulder, "Don't wait up!"

"I don't have shoes on," I say.

"Who needs shoes?" Ivy says, tugging on my hand so I'll keep up with her.

"We don't have any wine, or food, or a blanket—"

"We don't need any of that romance stuff, Mr. Romantic. I've got it covered."

"You planned this?" I ask as we make our way up a steep path lined with soft white sand.

She winks at me in the moonlight. "You're not the only one with a devious mind, Nolan. Just relax and enjoy the walk."

"Where we going?"

"You'll see. Now tell me all about your day today. I have a feeling you left a lot of things out when you were talking with Five at the pig party."

So I tell her the truth. I tell her maybe I wanted a boy and I was afraid to admit that. Afraid I didn't know how to be a good dad to a daughter. Afraid she'd fall out of love with me if I wasn't the guy she thought I was.

She doesn't seem surprised. Because she says, "I fell in love with the infamous Mr. Romantic first, Nolan. Because that's who you thought you were back then. But you were wrong when you said the name was ironic. You're very fucking romantic. You lost sight of who you were back at Brown. And you fell into some kind of alternate reality where Nolan Delaney was an asshole. But I never fell for that act. I saw through you. And yeah, bringing you back out of that façade was a pretty intense experience, but it was worth it. Because every day since our date back on Martha's Vineyard you've showed me your true self. I love this guy. And today, when I found out you spent the whole day with Five's girls trying to learn how to be a better father to our daughter, well, I fell just a little bit harder for your romantic side."

"Girls aren't what I thought." I sigh.

"What did you think we were?" she asks, her face twisted up in a smirk.

I shrug. "Confusing. But I love Bronte and I wouldn't trade her for anyone. I don't know if she's gonna be like Louise and Mathilda. Or like you. Or like Rory. Or Tori, or Ellie, or Cindy. But it doesn't matter. I hope she's... just Bronte. Whatever that means. Tea parties in playhouses or chasing pigs in tutus. Crazy adventures or pretty dresses. Pointy spears and hoods, and capes or ballet lessons instead of tee-ball. I don't think it matters."

"You know what?" she asks.

"What?"

"She can be all those things and still be a girl."

I smile, then break into a laugh. "Yeah. I guess I know that now."

"You always knew it, Nolan. Just like you knew people didn't call you Mr. Romantic because it was ironic. You're the most romantic man I've ever met. You just needed me and Bronte to help you get over the past and admit to yourself that you've always been a pretty nice guy."

We stop walking and I realize we're standing in front of a waterfall with a pool of sweet-smelling water rippling in the shine of moonlight. "Where are we?" I ask.

"We're at Five and Rory's secret spot. I told her I needed a date with you tonight and she said to bring you here."

"It's... fucking beautiful."

"But there's one more secret place she told me about. Come on, follow me." Ivy takes my hand and leads me over to some rocks. She says, "Climb, Nolan. I'm taking you to the top of the world."

I just shake my head and smile as I do as I'm told. And when we get to the top of the hill, we can see the whole island.

So perfect. So still. Such... paradise.

"This is my fantasy, Mr. Romantic." And then Ivy Delaney, my wife and soulmate, and mother of my child, unbuttons her blouse as it flutters in the hot, tropical breeze, and says, "Trust me. I'm gonna take care of you tonight."

So I do.

# CHAPTER TWENTY-EIGHT

# WEST

I have to wake Ethan up in the morning. He's dead asleep, snoring loudly in the second bedroom. Tory left an hour ago and put me in charge of wrangling all the guys together into some coherent group because the women were busy. "We don't have time to make sure you guys get to the altar, Weston," she said. "We had a wedding-dress crisis last night and we've all got to pull together to make this the best day ever."

So I mumbled out a sleepy, "You got it," and rolled back over, trying to forget the fact that I went lobstering yesterday without gloves and my hands are stinging like fuck.

But now that I'm fully awake, this shit is real. "Ethan," I say, shaking him for like the tenth time in nine minutes. "Get up. We've got things to do. We're getting married today."

I look down at my hands and realize I've got little pinpricks of blood all over my palms. So I go into the bathroom, looking for a first-aid kit so I can wrap them up.

He yawns cavernously, rubs his eyes, and says, "I can't be your best man, Dad."

"What?" I stop applying ointment to look over at him. "Why not?"

"Because then I'll be standing by you instead of Mathilda and Louise."

215

"OK," I say, not really understanding. Mathilda and Louise are the flower girls, I know that much. But... "Is that a bad thing?"

"Yeah," Ethan says, sitting up in bed. "Because we're kids, right?"

"Right." I still don't get it.

"Well, if I'm the only kid standing up there with you, when no one else has a best man, then I'm not really a kid. So I'm gonna carry the rings like little boys are supposed to."

Hmmm. I think about this for a second as I wrap my hands in gauze—if I get blood all over my shirt, Tori will kill me. None of the other guys have a best man because... well, we're all getting married on the same day. I'd always have had Ethan standing with me. But I'm pretty sure if we weren't all getting married on the same day, Pax and Oliver would be each other's best man, and Nolan and Mac would be each other's best man. And Five would probably ask his little brother Wyatt or his brother-in-law Jax, or his crazy Uncle James. But since none of the other guys had a best man, he's opted out too.

I realize we've all become pretty good friends over the last year. Sure, we spent a lot of time apart since everything happened back in college, but this last year was good for us. We're kind of a team now and that means we can't be both groom and best man to each other on the same day. So we decided Ethan would stand with me and no one else would have a best man because we just don't have enough people. And the parents didn't want to fill in. They wanted to be sitting in the front row watching.

"And," Ethan continues, "I kinda like Mathilda. She's fun."

"Oh," I say, laughing through my smile. I get it now. He wants to stand next to *her*, not me. "Well, I'm OK with that."

"Yeah," Ethan says. "I knew you would be. Plus..." He stops to look up at me. "Now you know for sure, right?"

"Now I know what?" I ask.

"That I've decided to be a kid again. I'm gonna hang out with Mathilda all the time now. She said she'd show me the ropes."

"Did she? Well, that's gonna be challenging, since she lives here and we live in Colorado."

"I'm not worried about it," Ethan says, jumping up from bed.

I ruffle his messy hair and say, "Me either, sport."

We grab our tuxes and head out, banging on all the bungalow doors as we make our way past. Pax is next door, so we grab him first. He's got tape across his nose. I think Five broke it last night because of the whole Charles Vance thing. Then Mac comes, with a huge bandage over the side of his neck.

"What the fuck is that?" Pax mumbles, pointing at Mac's neck.

"Fucking mutant bee stung me yesterday at the cave you told me to take Ellie to." Perfect glares at me for a second, but then points to Paxton's taped nose. "You deserved that."

"Fuck you," Pax grumbles.

We grab Nolan next. "What the fuck?" I ask him. "What the hell is wrong with your face?" He has a huge lump on the side of his head near his ear. A proper goose-egg with an ugly blue-green bruise that leaks onto his cheek.

Nolan touches it, winces, and says, "Got hit in the head with a rock while I was chasing down that baby pig."

We can't help but laugh as we picture how that must've went down.

I bang on Oliver's door and he comes out swinging his garment bag over his shoulder. His lip is split from where Five elbowed. He dabs at it with a tissue and says, "Don't say a fucking word," as he takes up the lead.

We meet Five up at the main house and take up residence in his living room to get dressed. He's got a beauty of a black eye from where Ariel clocked him.

We're a bunch of fuck-ups because we're gonna look like hoodlums in tuxes with all our injuries.

But... this might turn out to be the most awesome wedding picture ever.

# CHAPTER TWENTY-NINE

# PAX

I think Nolan is the most interesting part about watching everyone get ready for the wedding. Ivy had one of the Shrike sisters drop Bronte off about an hour ago with these simple instructions. "Make her pretty. Whatever that means to you."

I have to say… I'm jealous of that asshole right now. Five's girls are all over him. Even the twins. They give him hair tips and show him headbands and barrettes that might match Bronte's dress. Bronte, to her credit, is patient with her father. She sits quietly on a rug in the center of the living room sucking on a corner of a baby blanket as she watches everyone with drowsy eyes.

My nose hurts from that punch Five gave me last night. But I'm pretty sure his eye is throbbing just as bad. Not to mention my arm is killing me where Golden Balls bit me.

I look around the room as I straighten my tie. Every one of us looks nervous. Even Five. I walk over to him and say, "Hey, I really am sorry about last night."

He's tying his tie, looking at his fingers in the mirror as they work the knot. But he glances up at me and shrugs. "You didn't know."

"I could've told ya he was coming."

"Yeah, and I would've freaked out and probably said no." He turns to face me, offers up a small smile, then says, "And it's not my call, right? Who gets to attend your wedding. He's your father, Pax. If you want him here, he

219

should be here. And don't let anyone tell you otherwise." He claps me on the shoulder and walks off, calling out to his girls, "Out, ladies! We're T-minus ten minutes until take off. Go find your mother!"

Nolan hands Bronte off to his mother, and I swear, that guy's heart is gonna explode if the look on his face is any indication of how he's feeling.

I glance at Oliver in the mess of people and find him looking at me. He swallows hard and pushes past his father to make his way over. "Hey," he says.

"What's up?" I ask, smiling. "You nervous?"

"Nah," he says. "Just... I'm sorry, OK? About giving you shit. You're the right guy for her, Pax. And now... well, I can't think of a better man to call a brother."

I pull him in for a man hug. He claps my back and then we break away and sigh. "This is it," I say "The end of the crazy Mister life."

"You're not gonna lose your edge, Mr. Mysterious. My sister is safer with you than any other person on this planet."

"Thanks," I say. "It means a lot to me. I really do love her, Oliver. And I know she's tough, but keeping her safe is the only job that matters now."

"You've got it in the bag."

And then Five's father whistles sharply to get everyone's attention. The entire room calms down at his request. "It's time," he says. "Let's do it."

My stomach does all kinds of weird things as we file out of the house and make our way down to the beach. There's an open tent to keep the sun off us and a whole bunch of people. But I'm surprised to see photographers snapping pics as we walk.

"What the hell are they doing here?" I ask Oliver with a nudge.

"I guess Five finally gave up," he says. "He said they could come down to photograph the wedding if they promised not to circle the helicopters during the ceremony."

"Dude's got all the answers," I say.

"Yeah," Oliver admits with a sigh. "He really does. But he's fucking Five, so what'd I expect?"

We all walk up on the platform serving as an altar and Pastor Rockwell greets each of us by name as we take our places.

When the music starts, I seriously think I might throw up. But then there they are. Our girls, starting with Louise and Mathilda, who throw flower petals as they make their way up front. Ethan is behind them holding a long pillow with twelve wedding rings on top. All lined up in a neat little row. Ellie appears first and I have to take a second look at her dress, because that's not quite what I imagined as her style. It's got a long slit up both sides and she's showing a lot of leg. Then I notice Ivy has a similar dress and I know that's not her dress. When Tori comes out wearing a miniskirt I start getting excited at what Cindy might have in store for me. And then there she is... radiant. My Miss Cookie takes my breath away. It's not the dress. I barely have time to look at the dress as she comes towards me.

All I see are her eyes, staring up at me, as I lift her veil. She whispers, "You found me, Detective Mysterious."

I smile and say, "No, Miss Cookie. You found me."

"You're the real deal, Paxton Vance. A true Prince Charming."

I pretty much beam happiness as Pastor Rockwell
begins to speak.
But I can't stop looking at her.
I got a real-life Cinderella.
And she kicks ass.

# CHAPTER THIRTY

# OLLIE

I start smiling when I see the girls come out in their newly altered dresses. Ellie and Ivy have slits up the side that I'm pretty sure were not authorized by Ivy's father, because I catch him squinting at her bare legs.

Then Tory shows up in a miniskirt and I have to cover my mouth. Because I know what happened last night after Kat's dress got ruined by those vagrant kittens.

Cindy shows up in something so inappropriate for a wedding, she might as well wear that to her next rock concert. I'm pretty sure all the paparazzi have forgotten all about Charles Vance and every picture on TV tomorrow will be of my baby sister's legs.

But then I look at Paxton and he's not even remotely interested in what she's wearing.

Yeah, letting him off the hook for falling in love with Cindy was the right thing to do. Because he's a goner.

And then I see Katya. She looks scared and small compared to everyone else. She's very young, but in a different way than Ivy. And even though her dress is a patchwork of all the spare lace and satin and chiffon the other Mrses could spare, it's the most beautiful dress I've ever seen.

Because it was made with love. Every bride-to-be gave up a piece of her dress so my sisters and mom could make Kat a new one.

Katya is crying as she reaches for my hand. I squeeze her fingers and pull her veil away. "I love you," I whisper. "And that dress is beautiful."

She wipes her tears, not caring about her makeup. "I know," she says. "It's better than perfect. It's more than I ever imagined."

She gulps a huge breath of air, straightens her shoulders, and we turn together and face the pastor.

I don't hear a word he says. I don't even say the right vows when it's my turn to talk. I look at no one but Katya. I speak only to Katya. I make all my promises to her. And when we put our rings on we realize… it's done.

We made it.

I kiss her long and hard and she whispers into my mouth, "Kiss me here," as she points to her tattoo under her ear.

So I do.

"And here," she says.

I do again.

"And here," she says.

I hold her close and bury my face into the soft skin of her neck. And I kiss her… everywhere.

We've been through a lot, us Misters. But these girls came along with us. And they're still here. And we're still here.

It's fitting, when they take our picture after the ceremony is over, that we're just a bunch of banged-up guys. Black eyes, bee stings, split lips, bleeding hands, and broken noses.

We've made a lot of mistakes. We're not perfect by any means. But we know how to love.

And we're just like the dresses our brides are wearing.

Cut up into pieces, patched back together, and sewn up into something new.

Something better than we were before.

# CHAPTER THIRTY-ONE

# FIVE

It's funny how life can totally derail and go off track and you end up someplace you never thought you'd be.

I'm pretty sure Mr. Perfect never imagined he'd go out to my island and leave with a pack of kittens. But Ellie fell in love with them, so they took all five back to their little farm. I imagine a farm is pretty much a cat's dream. And I'm equally sure that Mrs. Perfect never imagined herself taking in a family of six orphaned siblings after their parents died in a car wreck and then find out a month later she's pregnant.

Nope. I was there for that and I can say with one hundred percent certainty, Mrs. Perfect never saw that coming.

Most people might send those foster kids back so they could concentrate on their own family, but Ellie and Mac just added on a few bedrooms to their house and never even blinked. It wasn't a challenge, Mac told me later. It was just a transition.

The best thing about their news was that a few months later Ivy—Fertile Myrtle that she is—got pregnant again, so they can have babies together now. Nolan's not rooting for a boy, he says. And while I might think that remark was disingenuous coming from, oh, just about anyone else, I don't think it is, coming from him. Because he told me, "I want girls just like you have, Five."

And I said, "What do ya mean?"

And he said, "Mathilda and Louise." He said, "They are perfect and I love them. And if I get two girls, they'll have the same age gap as your two. And I'll teach them everything it means to be a girl."

I don't doubt that at all. I think Nolan Delaney makes a fine girl. I caught him painting his nails last week and he just shrugged and said, "I got this color for Louise, but I'm trying it out to make sure it's sparkly enough. She likes sparkles."

Indeed she does.

Corporate got his kid under control. Actually, my daughter seems to have been the one to get his kid under control. I guess I can't fault the boy. Mathilda is already spectacularly smart, adventurous, sassy, and looks just like her mother. But now I know how Spencer Shrike felt about me at that age.

I wanna strangle Ethan Conrad and invite him in for a talk at the same time. Because that kid is cool as fuck.

So I'm rolling with that one. For now.

Tori had a girl, so she and West are regulars over here for Nolan Delaney's day-out-with-the daughters thing.

I just shake my head at that dude. Whatever.

Mysterious and Cindy took off for a round-the-world trip. We haven't seen them since the day after the wedding. But Cindy calls every weekend to talk to Rory and tell her where they're at, what they're doing, and send us pictures of themselves hanging off cliffs or swimming with dolphins, and all that other Airborne Ranger shit they do. I keep joking with Mysterious that he needs to get his ass back here and help me start a horse breeding business. But he always yells, "Fuck that Golden Balls asshole!" when I bring it up. Which I do often, just to hear him call Rory's prize pony that name.

Oliver and Kat live down the road now.

Oh, yeah. I forgot to mention we moved home. Home home. Like Shrike farm home. I'm fucking my wife in her childhood bedroom every goddamned night and there's nothing Spencer Shrike can do about it.

But Oliver and Kat found a farm down the road too, so they're down there now. Ollie took over Shrike Bikes and my dad is trying to get him to do a reality show.

My stupid dad.

But I think Ollie is into it. So we'll see where that goes.

Kat is a full-fledged Shrike Bitch now. She's working with my sisters and taking pictures of their new boutique downtown that specializes in one-of-a-kind handmade wedding dresses.

Ana and Isa both got into the school Rory wanted to send them to. They stay there during the week and come home on the weekends. I want to die of sadness every Monday morning. But every Friday night when they come home and tell me about their week, I grow stronger.

They will leave me for good one day. And they love their school down in Colorado Springs. And Ellie pops in twice a week to take them out to dinner. And Ivy takes them shopping every Wednesday afternoon.

I want them to stay little forever. And I'd take us back to the island in a second if I thought I had a chance to stop time and make it work. But I don't, so I get over it.

Turns out Mac was right when he said Colorado is the perfect place to be. I feel like... people know us here. They've got our backs. Plus, the paparazzi splashed our faces all over the TV for months. They had that pig video running with a play-by-play for each fucked thing that went wrong. It was like some kind of dissection of a NFL game. With little x's and o's drawn on the screen to show who went where, and blah, blah, blah.

We had something like sixty million views on one of the YouTube videos.

If anyone touches my girls, the world is gonna know about it.

So I guess that's it as far as this story goes. And yeah, it's funny how life can derail and go off track and you end up in a place you never thought you'd be.

But my life never went off track.

I got my queen, and my princesses, and my farm, and my family. I got a new pony for Mathilda since she grew too big for her last one. He's white and she calls him Snowflake, even though Rory and I never told her that story. And I'm pretty sure Rory is gonna make her a princess costume and Tory is gonna make Ethan a knight costume. And in a few weeks, they're gonna clip-clop through downtown Fort Collins and trick-or-treat on horseback.

Nope... my life never derailed.

Because I'm right where I was always supposed to be.

# End of Book Shit

I feel like I've written a lot of endings in 2017. I started the year with Taking Turns and wrote the end of that series in July. Then I picked back up in the Anarchy series and wrote the end of that series in June. Then there was Five. :) And that was an end and a beginning at the same time, which was a first for me. Not to mention I re-released the Dirty, Dark & Deadly series (Come, Come Back, and Coming for You) as a single book called The Company. Those books were a spin-off of the Rook & Ronin series, and even though it was and ending, it was also a beginning because Meet Me in the Dark and Wasted Lust came afterward.

So here we are now… the final Mister book that ties Five and Rory back to Mac, Nolan, West, Pax, and Oliver.

But is it an ending? I just got a tweet asking if I'll ever write books about the Rook & Ronin kids. And of course, people have been asking for the Vaughn brothers for a long time now. I don't know if I'll write a book about Kate, Sparrow, Ariel and the other kids that grew up with Five and Rory. Maybe. Maybe not. But I'll tell you who I think stole the show in this book… Mathilda and Louise! I had so much fun writing Mr. Romantic's parts. That little pig and those little girls just kinda made me happy I decided to do this book.

And Ethan… Jesus. If ever there was a kid who needed a grown-up book, I think it's him. I kinda have it in my mind that he's gonna fall for Mathilda the same way

Five fell for Rory. The same way Spencer fell for Veronica.

I have written two happily ever after books now (the first was for Rook & Ronin and is just called Happily Ever After) and I tell you what, they are a super fun. Yes, each of the guys had problems in this book, but they are relatable problems. No one got seriously hurt. No one was in serious danger. No one got a twisted fucked up crisis. Well, unless you count Kat's dress getting mauled by kittens. But I think Kat would agree with me when I say the new dress was better anyway.

So it's weird that 2017 was a year of endings for me. Because about halfway through the year I started talking to this guy named Johnathan McClain and that was nothing but new beginnings from the moment it started. He's an actor and a writer of screenplays and some of the most kick-ass poetry I've ever listened to (Yes, he recited (or more aptly, PERFORMED) a poem he wrote when he came to visit a few weeks ago). And he and I just kinda hit it off creatively.

We wrote a screenplay for The Company and we started pitching it as a TV series a couple weeks ago. (If you missed our announcement, he's also one of my audiobook narrators going under the pseudonym of Tad Branson). We started chatting on Twitter shortly after he narrated Mr. Romantic. I apologized PROFUSELY because I had loved him in other audiobook productions and begged my audio publisher to "get him" for me and I had no idea they'd ask him to be the Infamous Mr. Romantic. I'd asked for him to be Mr. Mysterious. But scheduling five men to narrate the Misters was difficult, so he got Mr. Romantic. Jesus. If I had known my favorite narrator (and soon-to-be friend) would have to narrate that fantasy rape, I'd probably never have written it. ;)

But after he narrated The Company he sent me the MOST AMAZING email. I can't even describe that email, it was just too awesome. But that ultimately led to us talking about writing the screenplay and from there... new beginnings just started pouring in for both of us. So... we're officially partners now. And we've got a lot of stuff coming up (which will all be announced next week in a video we're doing while we're both here in Vegas.) Some beautifully amazing things are happening.

So maybe 2017 is an ending after all. But believe me when I tell you, the new beginnings we have in store for you will make up for anything that ends. I promise.

So 2018 will start off with a spin-off series of The Turning Series. If you read those books then you'll remember a player called Jordan. And if you didn't read it, by player, I mean like a game player. Not a "player". Because he was an integral part of Bric's Game and guess what? Jordan has his own game going. So the next book, releasing January 16, 2018 (cover reveal and pre-orders links go up on November 13) is called Jordan's Game: Total Exposure. This is the first of a four-book standalone series about what Jordan was really up to in His Turn. All four books will release in 2018.

What? Only four books you say? For the entire year? Why JA Huss, what the ever-loving fuck are you talking about?

Shit, bitches. Four books? In one year? Please. ;) Hold tight... I've got news coming up on my blog on November 6th. News you won't want to miss, I promise. So go there and fill the little form at the bottom of this post to FOLLOW ME, and you'll get that news first. OR, you can just join my Facebook fan group (Shrike Bikes – just ask to join and someone will add you as soon as they see it) and watch the amazingness unfold there.

Either way, you won't want to miss what I've planned for you. And I think calling 2018 the year of new beginnings would definitely apply.

So that's it, I guess. The Misters are over but if I ever get an itch to come back to it, there's always Mathilda and Ethan to write about when they finally grow up.

We don't have anything definitive about The Company TV series yet, but Johnathan and I will keep you posted if there's an update that's worth sharing. I took most of 2017 off of book signings because I was buying a new house and needed to write a lot of books to do that, but I'm back in 2018. I'll be at RARE – London Calling in February, at Boston Talk Books Event in April, at book Bonanza in Denver in July, San Fran Golden gate Author Event in August, and Romancing the Coast Author Event in Australia in September.

So if you'd like to meet me in person, try and come to one of those.

Thank you. For all your endless support and love. And for going on this crazy, fucked-up Rook & Ronin, Company, Mister journey with me.

See you in the next book. And if you enjoyed this book (or any of my other ones) please feel free to shout it out to the world by leaving a review. I'd really appreciate that.

Julie
JA Huss

# About the Author

JA Huss is the New York Times and USA Today bestselling author of more than twenty romances. She likes stories about family, loyalty, and extraordinary characters who struggle with basic human emotions while dealing with bigger than life problems. JA loves writing heroes who make you swoon, heroines who makes you jealous, and the perfect Happily Ever After ending.

You can chat with her on Facebook, Twitter, and her kick-ass romance blog, New Adult Addiction. If you're interested in getting your hands on an advanced release copy of her upcoming books, sneak peek teasers, or information on her upcoming personal appearances, you can join her newsletter list and get those details delivered right to your inbox.

JA Huss lives on a dirt road in Colorado thirty minutes from the nearest post office. So if she owes you a package from a giveaway, expect it to take forever. She has a small farm with two donkeys named Paris & Nicole, a ringneck parakeet named Bird, and a pack of dogs. She also has two grown children who have never read any of her books and do not plan on ever doing so. They do, however, plan on using her credit cards forever.

JA collects guns and likes to read science fiction and books that make her think. JA Huss used to write homeschool science textbooks under the name Simple

Schooling and after publishing more than 200 of those, she ran out of shit to say. She started writing the I Am Just Junco science fiction series in 2012, but has since found the meaning of life writing erotic stories about antihero men that readers love to love.

JA has an undergraduate degree in equine science and fully planned on becoming a veterinarian until she heard what kind of hours they keep, so she decided to go to grad school and got a master's degree in Forensic Toxicology. Before she was a full-time writer she was smelling hog farms for the state of Colorado.

Even though JA is known to be testy and somewhat of a bitch, she loves her #fans dearly and if you want to talk to her, join her Facebook fan group where she posts daily bullshit about bullshit.

If you think she's kidding about this crazy autobiography, you don't know her very well.

You can find all her books on Amazon, Barnes & Noble, iTunes, and KOBO.

Made in the USA
Columbia, SC
30 October 2020

23721049R00145